# Life Entwined with Lily's

## Sherry Boas

Caritas Press

To Megan,
May you be
surrounded by
all that is true
and beautiful.

# Life Entwined with Lily's

Sherry Boas

Second Edition, 2011

10 9 8 7 6 5 4 3 2

ISBN: 978-0-9833866-2-9

Published by Caritas Press, Phoenix, Arizona

For reorders and other inspirational materials visit our website at LilyTrilogy.com

For Phil, who astonishes me, time and again, with his boundless generosity.

"The power of selfishness to destroy lives versus the power of self-giving love to restore hope is the theme of this amazing story … with profound relationships and moving symbolism and enough realistic detail to remind the reader of a similar drama in their own lives ... I hugged my nine year old daughter with Down Syndrome each time I reluctantly put the books down, and saw heretofore unappreciated qualities in my family. The Lily Trilogy filled my heart with gratitude for my family, and made me determined to be the catalyst of God's healing ... How many times can it be said that a novel makes you a more grateful, loving person..."         Leticia Velasquez, writer and media critic

"The Lily Trilogy so beautifully, candidly and, at times, humorously, captures the incredible sacrifices and unmatched rewards of parenthood. This is a story for all parents who struggle in one way or another. And isn't that pretty much all parents?"
Father Doug Lorig, creator of
*A Spirituality of Parenting* video series

"I could not put these books down. Ms. Boas captures the raw emotion and secret thoughts of the human heart and pours them out into novels which will make people think, question, and no doubt view the sanctity of every life with more value. The depth of the characters and the very real situations they encounter draw the reader into story lines that touch on every point of human life – from conception to death – with humor, tenderness and, above all, a realness sure to penetrate anyone lucky enough to find these gems."
Kristina L. Forbes, mother of seven and pregnancy
counselor trainer

"Sherry's writing is riveting! She possesses a rare ability to develop characters you *really* connect with; to make you laugh heartily in one moment and to reduce you to tears in the next; to reflect on your Catholic faith; to appreciate the dignity of every human person; to blindside you with unexpected plot twists; and to appreciate her artistry with the written word."
Very Rev. Fr. John Lankeit, Rector,
St. Simon & Jude Cathedral, Phoenix

# Contents

# 1

## Hating Swan Sea

None of us knew how to tell Lily about Pablo. We put it off so long, that we ended up not having to. The question became its own inverse. Not how do we tell Lily about Pablo, but how do we tell Pablo about Lily. Unlike the original question, the second had to be answered swiftly. He, after all, is her father. And although it's the last thing in the world any parent wants to hear, when some unthinkable horror befalls a child, pity the person who would delay telling the dreadful news. It is a parental right to suffer alongside the child.

Although Pablo was absent for the first three decades of Lily's life, he has more than made up for it in the last two. Pablo was there for Lily at the death of her beloved Auntie Bev, the woman who raised her because there was no one else to do it. Pablo flew in from Burbank and helped nurse Lily back to health after a hernia operation, taking a leave of absence and extending his stay for six weeks when infection set in. The following year, Pablo walked Lily down the aisle and gave her away to her beloved -- a 40-year-old man who also happened to have Down Syndrome. Four years later, Lily leaned into Pablo's sturdy frame and watched her husband's coffin descend into the ground. Pablo has been at every one of Lily's birthdays, since she found him nearly twenty years ago, except her 45th, when he

1

was in the hospital with pneumonia. Because of all of this, and for reasons no one would be able to explain, Pablo and Lily have one of those rare spiritual connections which manifests itself most readily through a combination of vocal cords and fiber optics. If Lily murmurs the name "Daddy," the phone rings and it's Pablo.

So it was mystifying, yes, but not the least bit surprising, that five weeks after Pablo told Mom that he had an inoperable brain-stem tumor, Lily was in the operating room having part of her skull removed in a procedure called a decompressive craniectomy, designed to alleviate the pressure in the brain following a massive stroke. The surgeon tucked the portion of the skull that he removed into a flesh pocket just under Lily's abdominal skin, aiming to preserve it until the brain swelling subsides enough to put it back. Fourteen days post-op, however, Lily developed a brain abscess, which proved resistant to antibiotics. She lapsed into a coma, surprising everyone when she awoke on the sixth day. Doctors determined she is completely paralyzed on her right side, that she will never walk, talk or eat again and that she is unaware of her surroundings in what is known as a persistent vegetative state. At the age of 55, Lily was sent home with a hospice nurse, a feeding tube, a three-inch diameter hole in her head and a piece of her own skull still tucked away in her belly.

We all know that if she could say a word, it would be "Daddy."

Against doctors' orders, and ours, Pablo is foregoing his last three weeks of radiation therapy to come and be with Lily.

"I am an old man, Mijita," he told me. "The good Lord has granted me more days than I deserve already. In my life, I have nothing to lose, except the chance to see my Lily again. My mind is firm, my sweet Beth. I am coming."

So we traded in the ticket we had purchased Lily four weeks ago, from Seattle to Burbank, for a one-way ticket from Burbank to Seattle. Pablo will be on that plane tomorrow.

I'll sit in the dark until then, listening to the labored breathing of an aunt whose life is slipping away slowly – or maybe quickly, God only knows. It's a life that saved mine and now I can do nothing for it, except adjust pillows and launder linens. I whisper things to her all day long in a desperate, self-conscious attempt to keep her company on the off chance she knows I am here.

I've grown to hate my walls. I've never noticed before how grey Swan Sea is. Mom said it was an optimistic hue of blue when she helped me and Lily choose it for the living areas. But now it makes me feel as if I am trapped within the lyrics of Paul Simon's depression. *Kathy, I'm lost, I said, though I knew she was sleeping. I'm empty and aching and I don't know why.*

I hate my clock too. A family heirloom, the antique Bulova taunts as it ticks. And I hate the refrigerator. It cuts on and off by its own will, humming and then not humming and then humming again, on and on and on, as if Aunt Lily were still able to open its doors and ravage its contents in the middle of the night when anyone who would caution her to watch her weight had gone to bed.

Lily and I have been roommates ever since last year, when I finished my veterinary science degree at the University of Washington. I didn't think Mom was ever going to let me have her. But she finally agreed that Lily and I share so many common interests, it was only logical. I had set up an art studio in the space above my garage, and Lily was spending countless hours with me painting in there and then crashing on the couch late at night. Plus, she had become one of our most dedicated volunteers at the animal shelter, and was offered a six-day-a-week job there. Moving her in with me saved me an hour driving every day. Aside from the logistics of it all, there was the emotional component. John would soon be going away to college. Lily's job of mother henning him was about to come to an abrupt halt, leaving her potentially more depressed at his parting. We didn't want to risk anything that would worsen her psychological state. Having the animals and the art supplies would be good distractions for her. And there turned out to be at least a couple of un-intentional side benefit to the plan. Having Lily live with me freed up another room for Mom and Dad to take in another kid. They have fostered more than three dozen children since they received their license just before John was born.

Out of all my mother's children, John is the special one to Lily. He's the one she helped raise from baby. She is the reason he exists. Knowing Lily could never have children of her own, Dad had a vasectomy reversal so Mom could get pregnant. I've never quite understood the extreme measures people will under-go to have babies. I have always resigned my own life to childlessness, quite certain I never want to be the one responsi-ble for bringing a child into a world that is capable of bringing so much harm to children. Every child Mom and Dad fostered came to us broken. Many could never be fixed. It wasn't until after I met Danny that I realized that, at the root of my aversion to motherhood is a deeply-held belief that I am not worthy of the love of a child. It is a logical conclusion. The darkness of my past looms like the shadow of a hideous creature at my back. There was a time when I thought it quite possible that Danny would be the only person in the world who could illuminate and eradicate the ugliness that has stalked me for some twenty years.

I don't remember all the details of our first date. But I do remember we talked about our mothers. Specifically about our mothers' tools. My mother has every power tool that Home Depot carries, all kept in dust-free condition in identical, transparent, air-tight plastic boxes, with their power cords coiled and fastened by twisty-ties, stacked in cubby shelves installed above her workbench. Also on the shelves is a stack of bright red plastic boxes, each dedicated to a specific household task. She has one marked "picture hanging," for instance. It contains a hammer, a level, a tape measure, two sharpened pencils, nails, hooks and wire. Her "bathroom make-over" kit contains grout, a putty knife, razor blade, caulking and a pumice stone. The "paint touchup" box has a brush, sponge applicator, stir stick, rag and plastic cup.

My mother's makeup drawer, on the other hand, is a complete disaster. Everything thrown in together, caked with foundation, flaking with dried mascara, the lipstick adhered to the eyeliner by a blob of nail polish. In all my childhood years, I never saw my mother purchase a single cosmetic. I am quite certain she wore lipstick from the very same tube for both my First Communion and my high school graduation. My mother was a stunningly beautiful woman, who had no need for makeup. She wore it only occasionally, like for weddings and funerals and childbirth.

"My mother was the handyman, too," Danny said, batting a fly away from his patty melt. "But she didn't have anything close to the setup your mother has. I don't know if we just couldn't afford a hammer, or she just thought they were redundant. But my mother pounded nails into the wall with the heel of her red stiletto pump. It was the only tool we ever needed. The makeup, on the other hand, that was a different story. That woman was stocked. And never even went out to check the mail without her seven layers of face. I always thought she presumed my father left her because she was not attractive."

"Was that why?"

"No," Danny said, taking another bite. "I think it was her cooking." His smile revealed dimples amongst the deep lines that were engraved by an abundance of time on ski slopes.

"You're terrible," I said.

"I'll tell you one thing, though, Beth. I don't doubt that your mother was stunning. She gave birth to the most beautiful woman I've ever seen."

This is the point where a woman will blush and a man will slide his hand across the table to touch hers. He'll lean in and allow his lips to lightly touch hers. He'll search her eyes for approval and then press his lips firmly on hers. Then he'll suggest that the sidewalk café is too noisy and they'll go for a walk. He'll point out something in a store window – a puppy or an antique easel or something -- pull her into a nearby alcove and pin her up against the wall, with a long, lusty kiss. None of this, however, happened between me and Danny.

"I think Lily needs a full work-up," he said, dipping his French fry in ketchup as a uniform delivery truck gravevelled past, its tires trying their hardest to grind dirt into the city's asphalt. "We need to see what's going on with her chemically. I'm going to order some blood tests."

"OK," I said. "Good."

"Has she always been pretty happy?" he asked. "You don't mind me talking shop, do you?"

"No, not at all," I said. "Yes, very happy. Aunt Lily, she's, well, you know, she's like a child. A happy child."

"It probably has to do with a change in body chemistry. Hormones, aging. The physical can all take a toll on the mental."

"A work up would be good," I said.

Aunt Lily turned out to have a low serotonin level. Danny recommended a mild anti-depressant and a diet rich in carbohydrates. I continued to drive her each week to her counseling appointments. Danny was always friendly toward me, but never asked me out again. After several months had passed, I assumed this meant our first date would be our last. I knew there had been something special between us, so I theorized he had gotten involved with someone else around the time we had eaten those hamburgers together. Or maybe we hadn't had a date at all. Maybe Danny had just wanted to discuss Lily. Or get some insight into her life or her family. I didn't know what to make of it, really. I also didn't know what to make of my heart pounding hard within my chest each time I pulled into the parking garage by his office.

# 2

## Symbolic Apples

Mom called from the airport to let me know she had gotten Pablo and they were on their way. I made one last sweep of the house, putting out a pair of mud-caked boots that had landed in the foyer, throwing out a paper plate full of sandwich crusts that had been left on the table from lunch, and gathering the wadded tissues that had spilled onto the floor from the pile on Lily's nightstand. I go through at least three boxes of Kleenex each week, in an effort to keep up with Lily's drool. I am vigilant about the cleanliness of Lily's chin, but I have to admit, I am not so much that way about my house.

My housekeeping skills have led many in my family to speculate that the real me was been abducted by aliens and replaced with a substitute who lacks the genetic material and lifelong conditioning that would allow her to call herself my mother's daughter or my grandmother's grandchild. Or my aunt's niece or sisters' sister, for that matter.

The germ phobia that has plagued our family for generations has somehow passed me over. It is difficult to harbor any fear whatsoever of germs when you spend your life caring for slobbery, smelly, flea-bitten strays. Doing so would surely lead to insanity. Mom was close.

I remember one time an heirloom soap dispenser that had been in the family for three generations fell into the porcelain sink and broke into more than a dozen pieces, cut Mom's index finger when she tried to clean it up, and broke the garbage disposal when a piece of it slipped down in and was unwittingly ground up. But the thing that most disturbed my mother was that she had just filled the dispenser with hand sanitizer and she had to stand helplessly by and watch a tragic portion of her germ-fighting arsenal ooze down the drain. Think of the millions of microbials that would never meet their end because of that little mishap.

I also did not inherit my mother's ability to organize. This I remembered as I stuck my hand down in my purse for my box of Altoids. I don't know why I never look into my purse until I have absolutely exhausted every possibility of finding what I'm look for via the Braille method. Probably because I can't see past the three months worth of old grocery lists, gum wrappers, deposit slips and cash register receipts. My hand always locates at least two other rectangular items before the Altoids. This time, it was a phone and a credit card case.

I needed an Altoid to settle my stomach. I needed to burp. On days like these, I think I must choke down my food and swallow too much air. I was dreading the doorbell, afraid for Pablo to see Lily. It couldn't possibly have any good affects on his condition. I was not expecting him to fall apart, but to suffer deep down, hard.

I was right. Pablo laid his head on Lily's chest and wept so that his body shook. Then he apologized to me and Mom and declared those his last tears. He came to uplift, he said, not to mourn. We must keep hope, he said.

"I know it's not easy, Pablo," Mom said, rubbing his shoulders. "Seeing her like this."

"At least she looks peaceful," he said, taking a hanky from his pants pocket. "I think one of the saddest days of my life, Beth, was when I heard that Frank had died."

"I know," I said. "He and Lily were so good together."

"That they were." Pablo's nose emitted a loud honk into his hanky. "My heart was broken into a million pieces for her. You'll know what I mean some day, Mija, when you have your own children. You feel their pain many thousands of times more than your own."

I smiled and squeezed his hand.

"It's times like these, Mija, when I ask the Virgin for help. She understands what it is like to watch a child suffer. Aih, how she understands."

The suffering of a child – the thought of that, the reality of that. That's what swept my mind away from the current moment at Lily's bedside to a legal document two decades into my past. I watched my signature, the first I had ever made, go onto the page, as if in slow motion. It looked large and childish – with bubble-shaped letters specific to teen-aged girls trying their best to be sophisticated.

"So tell me about this special man in your life, Mija." I was thankful that Pablo broke into my thoughts and rescued me from the remainder of that memory.

"I owe it all to Aunt Lily," I said. "I don't know if Danny and I would ever have had a second date if it wasn't for her coy and conniving ways."

I was not overstating that fact. One day, quite some time after that first date that never evolved into a second, Danny accompanied Aunt Lily out to the waiting room after her appointment. That usually meant he had received from her some important insight.

"What's for dinner tonight?" he asked, sticking his pen in his shirt pocket. "Lily invited me."

"I don't know," I said. "Aunt Lily is the cook in our house."

"I cooking meatloaf," Aunt Lily said.

"What time shall I arrive, Lily?" Danny asked.

"Six o'clock," she said. "No, 5:30. No 6:30."

"6:30?"

"6:30," Lily nodded. "Or 6. Jus- try no- be late. I very excited."

"OK, I'll be there at 6:15," Danny said. "Sharp."

"You two have fun," I said.

"Aren't you going to be there?" he asked.

"No," I said. "I have a date."

"With who?" Lily asked. "You don- have a boyfriend."

"Well, I have a date," I said, indignantly.

"I wan- Dr. Danny to be your date," Lily said.

I felt my cheeks get hot. I hoped he didn't see my blushing.

"Hey, that's not a bad idea," Danny said, grinning at me. "I think Lily is on to something."

"I might join you for dessert, OK Aunt Lily?" I said.

"No," she said. "I wan- you to eat meatloaf with Dr. Danny."

I looked into Danny's eyes and felt a magnetic pull.

"Oh, OK," I said. "I'll be there."

Danny was still grinning at me.

After dinner, Lily and I showed Danny our art studio. Lily wanted him to see her half-finished painting of a boat sailing under an orange moon. She has branched out in the last several years. She used to paint only wildlife, but will now do an occasional landscape. The boat painting was inspired by a harbor cruise our family took on Lily's birthday. Danny raved. Then his eyes fell on a painting of an old woman, looking pensively into the bushel basket she is holding. If you look closely, you can make out the reflection of a skull in each shiny red apple.

"I find this one really intriguing," Danny said, cocking his head and squinting at the unframed canvas. "What does it mean?"

"What do you think it means?" I asked.

"Hey, that's my line, Miss Lovely. Come on. Leave the Rorschach tests to us professionals, and just tell me what is the point of your painting."

"The old lady pick apples to make pie for her family," Lily said.

"But she sad because she don't have flour."

"That's a good interpretation," said Danny. "Now let's hear Beth's."

"I'm afraid you would have me committed if I told you," I said. "Come on, let's see what Lily made for dessert."

"Well, I know you're trying to change the subject," Danny said. "So let's hope she didn't make apple Betty."

"You're cute," I told Danny, ruffling his hair.

"Very cute," Lily confirmed, fixing his hair back again.

"You're beautiful," he told Lily, kissing her on the cheek. "And so is your impossible niece."

Over lemon cake, Danny floated a number of theories as to the message behind the old lady with the apples.

Wow," I said. "I've never had a painting inspire so much speculation."

"I'm more interested in understanding the artist," Danny said. "Are any of my interpretations close?"

"Nope."

"OK," he said. "Here goes my last shot."

"The elderly lady represents the aging process, which sneaks up on all of us. If it wasn't for the skulls on the apples, reminding her that she will one day die, she wouldn't even realize she is old."

"Nope."

"Not even close?"

"Not even close."

"Do the apples have something to do with the Garden of Eden?"

I decided to relieve Danny's suspense. He had labored enough.

"OK. It was widely known at my high school that if any girl needed an abortion, she was to go and see the home ec teacher. Mrs. Reiner would provide transportation to the clinic and hold the girl's hand during recovery. She would even help with funds, if need be. This way, a girl would never have to tell her parents that she was carrying their grandchild."

"Oh, I see. So, the old lady is Mrs. Reiner."

"It's been like twenty years since high school," I said. "So I guess Mrs. Reiner would be in her 70s by now. It's just hard to imagine a sweet elderly lady having been a part of something so covert. I tried to make her face as endearing as possible. Just to show the paradox of it all. A caring teacher, erasing children from the future."

"And each apple represents the death of an unborn baby?" said Danny.

"Yeah, according to my imagination," I said. "I'm sure no one but she knows how many she assisted with."

Two of my friends were beneficiaries of Mrs. Reiner's aid. My best friend, Caroline, had to call on her three times for help. I, however, never needed Mrs. Reiner.

After dessert, Lily fell asleep sitting up on the couch. I told Danny she often dozes off like that. He said that could be due to chemical imbalance. Or maybe she just needs more sleep. Perhaps sleep apnea is preventing her from getting quality REMs.

I fully expected, when I walked Danny to the door, that he would put his arms around me and kiss me for quite a long time. But he simply put his hands on my shoulders and gave me a quick kiss on the cheek, the kind he had given Lily in the art studio.

"Thank you for ditching your date for me," he said, placing his hand on the doorknob.

"Oh, it was no problem to reschedule," I said. "Good night, Danny."

I was hoping that comment would inspire him to get himself on my calendar.

"Goodnight, Miss Lovely. Lovely, Lovely lady."

ᎷᏆᏟᎡᏟᎷᏆᏟᎡᏟᎷᏆᏟᎡᏟᎷᏆᏟᎡ

Pablo spent several hours a day reading Lily's favorite books to her. Ever since she was 11, she has always been hooked on the Magic Tree House series, which were written for adventure-loving second graders who enjoy historical fiction. Pablo claimed to see a calm overtake Lily when he read. The rest of us were unable to detect it. But I don't doubt Pablo.

When Pablo wasn't reading to Lily, he was talking to her. About all kinds of things. Dog breeds, childhood, holidays, the saints, sporting events, gardening, family. I've never known someone so adept at one-way conversation. I figured by now Pablo would be longing for something from Lily in return, so I went into the art room and retrieved a rectangular package, wrapped in brown paper, taped messily at the corners.

"Pablo, Lily made this for you." Lily had planned to take it with her when she visited Pablo, but she had her stroke three days before she was scheduled to fly to Burbank.

I will never forget the look on Lily's face the day we presented her with the airline ticket and she finally understood what that little piece of cardstock she held in her hands meant.

"What it say?" She handed it back to Mom. "Read it."

"OK," Mom said, picking her reading glasses up off her chest, where they dangle from a chain. She put them on, tipped her head back and stretched the ticket as far away from her eyes as she could get it. "It says, 'Sea to Bur, Mar 29, UA flt 467, 3:45 p.'"

"What does that mean?" Lily asked.

"It means you're going to Burbank, California," Mom said handing the tickets back to her. "To see Pablo."

Lily's face was overcome with a jubilation usually reserved for the lame who discover they are suddenly able to walk. She jumped up and down, clapping and laughing, and said, "Yeah! I get to see Daddy! I get to see Daddy! I going to paint him a picture." And off she ran to the art studio.

Pablo carefully pried the tape up at one corner and slid his finger along the length of the opening until it reached the other corner. When the paper was peeled away, a simultaneous smile broke out on both our faces. It was a bull terrier, the kind of dog that Pablo gave to Lily to surprise her on her 35th birthday. It was sitting, staring at you with its large eyes, circled in brown.

Its head, cocked just slightly, was too big for its body, like a bobble-head in two dimensions.

"Oh, Lily, I love it! I am going to cherish it forever, Mijita." Lily just stared, blankly.

Mom had offered Pablo a room at her house, but he opted for my couch in order to be closer to Lily, whom we had set up in the family room. I initially refused to let Pablo sleep on the sofa, but he told me he would leave if I made him take my room. So Bruce had to relinquish his spot on the couch and climbed into bed with me. That animal has come a long way.

After Lily had her stroke, Bruce refused to come out of the corner of his kennel. Lily was the only one he fully trusted. The German Shepherd mix came to us badly mistreated, with visually countable ribs and ears singed by cigarettes. Standing at the kennel gate, I tried numerous times to get him to come to me, but he just raised an eyebrow and set his sad eyes on me, lacking the strength or the will or both.

I decided, one day, to take him home to see Lily. I had to carry him to my car. Once inside the house, he went straight for Lily's bedside. His muzzle just barely high enough to nose over her bed, he sniffed at her fingers, wagged his tail and let out a soft whimper. I picked up Lily's limp hand and placed it on Bruce's head, hoping as much as Bruce that the feel of his fur would inspire a scratch. Lily just blinked in her usual way. Her hand fell forward slightly and her fingers lay there lifeless as sausages on top of his long snout. Bruce was perfectly still and might have stayed there indefinitely had I not relieved him of his faithful anticipation and built him a bed of pillows on the couch.

"Remember how surprised you were when I gave you that puppy, Lily?" said Pablo, kneeling to give the German Shepherd a rub on the head. Pablo's hair -- what was left of it after several rounds of radiation -- had all gone grey. "He was a cute little dog, Lily. Remember? What did you call him? What was his name, Mija? Remember? You named him after greatness. Pablo Puppy. Remember, Mija?"

Bruce thumped his tail once and raised an eyebrow to look into Pablo's eyes.

"You're a nice animal too, Bruce," Pablo told the dog, easing himself onto the floor to sit beside him. "And you too are named for greatness."

"He is?" I said.

"Why sure. There was Bruce Lee. Bruce Springsteen. Bruce, the great white shark that starred in the movie Jaws."

"And don't forget Bruce Wayne," I said.

"Oh, yes."

"Danny's a big Batman fan."

"When am I going to meet this Danny of yours?" he asked.

"He's coming home tonight. He's been at a conference in L.A. for a few days."

It seems like much longer. Danny's not the kind of person you can be away from for too long without feeling the ache. Ever since the beginning, it's been that way for me. I hate it when he leaves. I never know if he is going to come back. That's a new one for me – something I've never had to worry about before. Men always come back – at least until they have taken you to bed. Which Danny has not done – quite intentionally on his part.

One evening, Danny and I had just come home from dinner and he was saying goodbye to me in my foyer, as he always did. We had seen each other for three months, and he had remained a perfect gentleman. I felt it was time to further our relationship. So, I grabbed his arm and pushed him up against the wall with the whole length of my body. I kissed him deeply.

"Stay the night with me," I whispered in his ear.

"I've got to go, Beth," he said.

"Danny, don't you want to be with me?"

"Not that way, Beth."

"I don't understand you," I said. "Have I just been imagining all of this chemistry between us?"

Danny smiled. "No, you haven't." He took me by the hands.

"Come on," he said, leading me into the kitchen. "I've been putting off this talk long enough. Why don't we brew some coffee."

The kitchen was dark, except for the under-cabinet halogens, which cast a warm glow on the mottled-brown granite counters. The lighting would have contributed to the romance, but I was too busy bracing myself for the big break-up speech. You're a great girl, but I'm not ready for a commitment. You're a great girl, but our lives are headed in two separate directions. You're a great girl but my heart belongs to someone else. This was strange timing, though. Usually this talk comes after the guy has slept with you.

"Don't you want to spend the night with me, Danny?" I asked, scooping seven tablespoons of Seattle's Best into the coffee maker.

"No," he said. "Well, yes, I do. But not this way. I don't want to just spend the night with someone. I want to spend my life with someone."

I let out a nervous chuckle. "Well, let's just take it one night at a time," I said. "Starting with this one." I pressed my lips on his.

"No, Beth," he said, gently pushing me away. "Look, here's the deal. As corny as it may seem. A long time ago, I decided the next woman to share my bed would be my wife."

He paused for my reaction. I just stared at him.

"So, I can't spend the night with you," he continued. "Not until you are my wife."

"Your wife?" I asked.

Danny just stared into my eyes.

"Are you--. Are you asking me to--. You're not asking me to--. Are you?"

"Only if the answer might be yes," he said. "Otherwise, I'd have to agree that it's too soon to ask."

"Yes," I said. "I think it's far too soon to ask."

"Darn," he said. "But point taken." He winked.

I smiled at him and kissed him on the lips again. He turned his head and hugged me tight into his muscular chest.

"So, what was tonight going to mean?" he said. "Anything?"

"I just wanted to be with you, Danny," I said. "I wanted to share something special with you."

"Someday, lovely Lovely Lady. God willing, someday."

# 3

## The Importance of Tripe

Pablo made sure Lily's bedside table always had fresh flowers. This he accomplished by putting $10 in my hand every time I went to the store and asking me to buy whatever flowers look the nicest, especially if they were orange, red or yellow.

"These, Lily," he said with a broad smile, upon seeing what I had brought home this time. "These were the favorite flowers of your great grandmother. These are called geraniums. And this was the color she loved." They were a red-orange, almost iridescent. "Your grandmother could grow anything. She had a very humble house with a very small garden. But her garden, it was overflowing always with flowers. Beautiful, beautiful flowers. People passing by would stop to look at them. And you know, your great grandmother -- that would be my grandmother on my father's side -- she had no money to buy flowers. It was hard enough putting food on the table. So whenever she did a job for someone, she would ask if she could take a little sprig or a little shoot or maybe a seed from their garden. That's how much she loved flowers. But the people who gave them to her, they were honored and always very generous. And there was another way she got her flowers. All her friends and neighbors, they would come to her door with dying plants and she would take them and bring them back. They would bloom like nobody's business. Oh,

Lily, there are so many things I've never told you." Pablo picked up her hand and kissed it tenderly. "There are so many things."

Lily just stared. Pablo stared too, out into the same space Lily was staring.

"I never got to tell you, Lily, that you have another sister. She died many years before you were born. She was a sweetheart, like you. You would have been good friends. Oh, I still miss her, Mija. She was the laughter in my smile, just like you."

I was in the kitchen putting away groceries. I stopped, a box of Ronzoni in each hand, waiting for Pablo to continue. I really wanted to know what happened to his daughter. And who was her mother?

I thought it strange that Lily had a sister she never knew. What games would they have played together? What would they have talked about? Would they share the same taste in clothes? Would they share anything at all?

I wondered if I should make it known to Pablo that I was hearing his conversation, so I could ask him questions. Just as I had decided I shouldn't, I heard myself blurt out, "How did she die?" I had abandoned my groceries, even the perishables and the ice cream, and was standing in the doorway.

A look of sorrow passed over Pablo's face and then he smiled at me, so I wouldn't feel bad for asking.

"It is a very long story. I will tell you sometime."

I knew this meant that no one would probably ever know. "Sometime" never really comes in any kind of a timely manner, and death would most probably precede it for a man with a terminal illness. But it was really none of my business anyway. Pablo and I share no biological ties, so his daughter I never knew is of no relation to me.

Mom and her brother Jimmy were adopted by Jen Eagan, before Lily was born. Then Pablo and Jen became lovers, and Lily was conceived. Jen broke off all ties with Pablo after Lily was born. She believed Pablo was unfaithful to her during her pregnancy, but Pablo insists Jen had jilted him before he moved on to another relationship. It's a move he says he regrets even to this day. Had he not tried to find comfort in the arms of another woman, he might have stood a chance at having a part in Lily's entire life, instead of just the last two decades. Mom, Uncle Jimmy and Aunt Lily were all raised by Jen's sister, Auntie Bev, when Jen died of cancer. Nobody even knew of Pablo until Lily was recovering from an accident some twenty years ago. Mom was trying to jog Lily's memory of her past and showed her a photo album that had a picture of a one-year-old Lily with a puppy. It was explained to her that her Daddy had brought the puppy to play with her for her birthday. Lily demanded a reunion. The Daddy turned out to be a school janitor named Pablo Perez. I can't imagine life without him now, but we all came very close to never knowing him. I suppose if Lily hadn't stepped out in front of that bus, nobody would have ever tracked him down. Auntie Bev had promised her dying sister not to. But Mom had made no such promise, so she was at liberty to embark on a search. It is the fruit of that search that inspired me to set about finding my biological grandmother, who lost her parental rights when she left Mom and Jimmy, sick with the flu, in their crib all night while she went out to get high. I was able to pay a small fee to a people finder and learn that she resides in a nursing home in Garden Grove, California. Before Lily had her stroke, I had been hatching a plan to sit face to face with her and ask some questions.

But for right now, my time is preoccupied.

"Oh, Mija. I wish. I wish. I wish."

"What do you wish, Pablo?" I asked.

"I wish I had many things to do over again.

"Some things just aren't meant to be, Pablo."

"Meant to be. Hmmm. Many things that are meant to be never are. Because of our weakness, or our pride or our stupidity. Or a combination of two or more of the above."

We sat in silence for a few minutes as I contemplated the truth in those words.

"Speaking of meant to be, where's that handsome fellow of yours been hiding out lately, Beth?"

Danny had come by once to meet Pablo after returning from his conference. He stayed only about an hour and said he had to go prepare a briefing for the others in his office.

"I think he's allergic to relationships," I told Pablo. "Or just plain scared."

"Scared? What would a handsome, accomplished, good-natured guy like him be scared of?"

"Intimacy." I said. "He's been hiding behind his ideals, but I've come to the conclusion, it's all just an excuse. He doesn't want to take our relationship to the next level. He wants to keep me at an arm's length. He's afraid of getting too attached. For some reason, I don't know why. I haven't given him any reason to fear me, but he is afraid."

"Has he said he doesn't want to see you?"

"No, he just doesn't want a physical relationship."

"Aaah, he is a wise man as well as being good-looking and accomplished."

"Wise?"

"Yes, Mija. Very wise. Ninety percent of the world's troubles would be over if every man was so wise. Men destined for greatness, throughout history -- from King David to Bill Clinton and many others who have come before and since -- have been brought down by their own uncontrolled passions."

Danny had told me three weeks before Lily's stroke that we should take a break from seeing each other, to try to ascertain, from a detached vantage point, what possibilities our relationship may have. This I took to mean that he was through. I surmised that he lacked attachment to me and didn't know how to tell me. Anyone who was madly in love would not be able to bear the separation. Danny was most certainly not madly in love with me. Though he toyed with the idea of marrying me, he hadn't even told me he loved me. I, meanwhile, had never felt such an intense bond to another human being, not counting my first love in high school. Because of this, I had decided not to resume a relationship with Danny, even if he might ask. It was too difficult never knowing where you stand with him, and I didn't want my heart messed with.

I might not have had an occasion to speak to Danny again if it wasn't for that horrible day. I had to say the words, but I was scared to hear them spoken. Mom was doing most of the notification of family and friends, but I had to be the one to call Danny.

"Danny? This is Beth."

"Beth, how are you?"

"Danny –"

"What is it Beth? What's wrong?"

"Lily," I said. "Lily has had a stroke."

"Oh, Dear Lord," he said. "What's her condition?"

"Not good, Danny."

"Where's she at. I'll come."

"Harborview."

When he arrived, he threw his arms around me and asked for an update. I told him she had gone into surgery and was not expected out for several hours. He told Mom how sorry he was. Then he took my hand and said, "Come on, let's go." He led me to the chapel, took rosary beads from his pocket and knelt. I knelt beside him. He wrapped his arms around me from the back, so the rosary was dangling from his hands in front of me. We prayed in silence. I watched his fingers move over the beads at the same pace I was saying my Hail Marys. We were somehow synchronized. How I remembered that prayer, I don't know. I hadn't said it since I was a kid.

The door opened behind us and neither one of us looked. Soon, Mom was kneeling next to us. She held her red rosary with the gold crucifix in her hands. Danny extended one of his arms and hugged her in tight to us. I have never felt this before, so I can't really tell you what it was, but the closest I can come to describing it is to call it a deep friendship, a oneness with another soul. And that's the way it stands to this day. What more it may become, neither one of us knows.

ฅ)ꚍ(ભฅ)ꚍ(ભฅ)ꚍ(ભฅ)ꚍ(ભฅ)ꚍ(ભ

There are two family recipes that Pablo has his heart set on passing on to me and my sisters: menudo and tamales.

"I always intended to show them to Lily because she loved to cook," Pablo said. "You just always assume you are going to have tomorrow with the ones you love."

"What is menudo?" I asked.

"It's a soup of celebration. We had it at Christmas or at Baptisms and First Communions. You know. All the great occasions. And to cure hangovers."

"What's in it?"

"Tripe, hominy, cow or pig's feet and red chile paste."

"Tripe?"

"Stomach."

"Oh. Maybe we should do tamales first."

"That is probably wise, Mija. Menudo is a delicious meal, but the preparation of it is not for the faint-hearted. The tripe has to be cleaned very well and it smells – let's just say – not so beautiful. You can lose the contents of your own stomach while cleaning out the cow's."

"Do you have to use tripe and feet? Can't you use chicken or something?"

"You can, of course, but then it's not menudo. Cow's stomach and feet. It's all the poor have. So the peasants, they make the best of it. But menudo is more than a soup. Menudo is an event. It brings people together. It takes hours to make, so everyone gathers into the kitchen and helps. The kitchen is where family love is at its deepest, Mija. Aside from funerals."

"Do you want to do menudo soup? We can try it."

"No, no, Mija," he said with a chuckle. "Not menudo *soup*. Just menudo."

"Well, isn't it soup?" I asked.

"Well, yes, it's soup, but you don't call it soup. You call it menudo. Calling it menudo soup is like calling clam chowder "clam chowder soup.""

"Got it," I said.

"Let's see, tamales or menudo?" He tapped his bottom lip lightly with is index finger. "Let's make tamales. I've had them every New Year's Day since I can remember. But I won't be around for another New Year's, so I better get my fill now, right Mijita?"

"Tamales it is," I said, forcing a smile, trying to ignore the rationale for his decision. "I'll get a shopping list from you as soon as I set up a date with Katie and Laura."

"And your mother, of course."

"Oh, yes," I said.

"I hope I can remember how to do it. I haven't made them for quite a few years, since my neighbor, Mrs. Ruiz, was widowed. She makes very tasty tamales and brings them on New Year's Eve. We share the evening together, with a couple other ladies from church, and my old friend Father Tomas, and we watch the ball drop on Times Square."

"Is Mrs. Ruiz your girlfriend?"

"Oh, Heavens no. I'm too old for one of those." Pablo flashed a warm grin. "And if I had one, I wouldn't call her Mrs. anything."

"What would you call her?"

Pablo looked out into his distant past. "I would call her 'mi amor, mi vida.'"

His eyes were a soft brown, nestled deeply into a foundation of wrinkles and creases. I felt as if something was pulling me into the very root of his soul. It was a beautiful place. I wished I could have stayed indefinitely.

Pablo got up with a considerable amount of effort, kissed me on the top of the head and slowly moved to Lily's bedside. He picked up her limp, rubbery hand and kissed it. I went to the kitchen to fix Pablo a cup of decaf Nescafe. When I returned, he was sitting at the foot of Lily's bed, humming to her a tune I had never heard, but instantly liked.

"Here's your swill, Pablo," I said.

"Those who haven't tried something should not pass judgment on it, Mija. Here, have a sip."

"I will eat the lining of a cow's stomach, if you want me to, Pablo. But I would never let instant coffee even touch my lips, even for you. Have you forgotten how long I have lived in Seattle?"

"A whole city of coffee snobs," He stood up and stretched with one arm, carrying his mug in the other hand. "I think I better get over to your nice comfortable sofa, Mija. My back is starting to hurt."

Pablo limped for several steps and then stood up a little straighter with each step. By the time he was completely erect, he had gotten to the couch and had to lower himself again.

"Can I get you your pain pills, Pablo?"

"No, no, Mija. I'm OK." He patted the cushion beside him.

"Come sit with me. You are better than any medicine."

We sat there for a little while, holding hands as Pablo drank his coffee.

"Pablo, what really happened between you and Jen?"

"What really happened?"

"Yes, there are stories, but they never really made that much sense to me. Do you mind me being nosy?"

"I take it as a compliment, Mija," he said, wrapping his arm around me. "You and me, we can tell each other anything, eh?"

"Yeah," I said, smiling. I didn't want him to suspect there was something I could never tell anyone.

"Well, I'm going to give you the whole story, Beth. You are the first to know the whole story. It is not one I'm proud of, but maybe someone can learn from it and be all the wiser for having heard it."

Pablo adjusted the pillow behind his back, poked his red and blue plaid shirt into his pants with his thumbs and leaned his head back on the couch. He closed his eyes as if watching his past replay itself on a screen inside his head. When the condensed, 15-second recap was over, he opened his eyes and spoke.

"After it became clear to me that Jen did not want to marry me, I was hurt. Probably as much in my ego as my heart. I felt I wasn't good enough for her, even though I had fathered her child. I was just a janitor. Poor, uneducated. So when another woman at the paper showed interest in me, I jumped at it. In the mind of a foolish young man, that woman's affections proved that I was good enough."

"I can understand how you could think that way," I said.

"Well, the big problem was that the woman who paid me the attention was Jen's best friend, Cali Flannery."

"Wow," I said.

"At first, it was my heartache that brought Cali and me together. She was a person who could give me advice. She was a person who could offer me comfort. Before we knew it, we had turned it into something more."

"She fell for you."

"Yes, and I fell for the distraction, but never for her. My heart still belonged to Jen. Always and forever more. To Jen."

"You never married?"

"There never was anyone else like Jen. I kept waiting. But no one else ever came."

I laid my head on Pablo's arm, which he had stretched out on the back of the couch.

"That's why it pains me to see people in love let a little thing come between them."

"What if it's not a little thing? What if it's a very large thing?

"Oh, Mija. Compared to love, all things are little."

# 4

## Con Los Angeles

Danny came over Sunday for dinner. Afterward, we went for a walk, while Pablo read Lily the sports news.

"It's such a beautiful night, Danny," I said, gazing up at the moon. "Let's go to your place."

"I like it here, Beth. I really like Pablo. He adds a great deal of warmth to your life."

"I just want to be alone with you, Danny."

"I don't think that's a good idea, Beth."

I pulled on his hands, stopped him in the moonlight, and hugged him, pressing hard against him. We hadn't kissed since he had called a timeout in our relationship, before Lily's stroke.

"You know what would happen, Beth," he said, pulling himself apart from me.

"It's really all I have to give," I said, "and I want to give it to you."

"No, Beth," he said, clenching his jaw. "You have a lot more to give. I don't want a piece of you, Beth. I want all of you. If I can't have that, I don't want any of it."

"If you really knew what you were asking for, you wouldn't be asking," I said.

"Beth, I am a shrink, and you've got me completely baffled. If I had to guess I'd say it's fear overtaking you."

"Fear over taking *me*? Danny, just out of curiosity, how did you come to your decision? About, you know, not sharing your bed."

"Well, that's a very long story," he said, taking my hand and pulling me along gently so we would resume our walk. "If I go into that, we actually will end up spending the night together, because it will take until morning to have that conversation."

What Danny proceeded to tell me, with a considerable amount of urging, on my front porch, over a pot of coffee, changed the answer I had given him about marrying him. I felt a pain stab through me like a sword had cut me lengthwise. I realized I couldn't even consider saying yes. Ever. No matter how long he might wait.

"When I was in my late 20s," he said, rocking us back and forth on my porch swing, "my girlfriend of three years snuck off and had an abortion. I only found out because I overheard her talking to a friend on the phone about it. I asked her why she did it and she just kept saying she wasn't ready to be a mother. It never crossed her mind that that was my child too. In the final analysis, though, I realized that what happened was as much my fault as it was hers. She's the one who had to make that awful decision, but it was because of a decision I had made to sleep with her in the first place. I started thinking how ridiculous the world is. Men running around, impregnating women, not even knowing it sometimes. I mean who knows how many children I may have out there – some of them alive, some of them dead. I wasn't exactly a paragon of virtue in my younger days. Those one-night stands, who knows? What if I have children I've never even met. It's weird being a guy, Beth. I just can't take the chance any more. Not to mention the suffering it brings to women. And their children. I just can't be part of that."

"So you swore off all premarital sex?"

"Yup."

"Wow."

"It actually hasn't been that difficult. Sarah was the only one I was ever really emotionally attached to. After she did that to me, I found it very difficult to trust anyone again. Basically, I've been keeping everyone at arm's length."

"Ah-ha! I knew you were afraid of relationships."

"Afraid of relationships? I'd marry you tomorrow if you said yes. You're the one who's afraid."

"Do you trust me?"

"Well, yeah. I do."

"Danny, I don't think that's such a good idea."

"Why?"

"It's just not."

"Tell me why, Beth. Why are you untrustworthy?"

"Well, I would never be the type to abort your baby without telling you, but there are some things you don't know about me. Some serious things."

"So, tell me."

"No. They are not things I can tell anyone. They are things that will actually make it impossible for you to have what you want with me. I can be your girlfriend, Danny, but I can't be your wife."

"Why?"

"It just can't be long-term, Danny."

"Beth, do you love me?"

Tears stung my eyes and I turned my face away from him. He turned my chin back toward him. "Do you, Beth?"

"I don't want to lie to you, Danny."

"Then, tell me." He grabbed me around the waist, hugged me tight and kissed my hair. "Oh, Beth, I missed you so much when we weren't seeing each other. Didn't you miss me?"

"Yes," I said. "I am very fond of you, Danny. Very attached."

"Then why can't we work towards something long-term?"

"Because of something in my past. That's all I will say, Danny. I won't tell you any more."

"Leave the past in the past, Beth. I'm only asking for your future."

"I'm sorry, Danny," I said. "I can't give you that."

"Why, Beth?"

I drew a long, heavy breath.

"I can't have children," I said. "And I'm sure you really want children."

"That's OK," he said. "We can adopt."

"No," I said. "I can't be a mother. I – don't want to be a mother."

"Oh," he said. He looked stunned and worried. He hugged me tight and gave me a kiss on the forehead.

I told him I had a sudden stomachache and asked if we could call it a night. I watched him in the moonlight as he got into his car. His tall, lean body was enshrouded in Seattle fog, or maybe it was just sadness. He is an extremely desirable man, I thought. A rare combination of all things good. And because of one solitary day in my past, I will never have him.

Pablo was still awake, sitting in the dark, when I came in.

"What are you doing up?" I said, standing behind the couch, rubbing his shoulders.

I heard tears in his voice. "I want to talk to Lily."

"Me too," I said.

He wiped at his eyes with the heel of his hands. "Danny go home?"

"Yup." I plopped beside him on the couch and he put his arm around me. We sat in the dark, our heads tipped back, staring at the ceiling.

"Do you ever regret not getting married?" I asked.

"Well, Mija, I actually was married once. Before Jen. You remember I told you once that Lily has a sister."

"Yes."

"I will tell you the story because you and your family are my only family. This information is important and should not die with me. The memory of my daughter – and her mother – should live on. So I will tell you."

He went on to chronicle a tragedy that made me wonder how a man lugging such a horrible history could get up every day and walk.

Pablo was a young man when his four brothers-in-law made it to America, and within two years time, managed to earn $3,000 to send back home. Pablo's mother-in-law determined it should be used to pay a coyote.

So 22-year-old Pablo, his 19-year-old wife Rosa, and their 2-year-old baby, Carmen, crammed into a windowless un-air conditioned fifteen-passenger van with three coyotes and eighteen other migrants, bound from Guaymas to Arizona, considering themselves fortunate to be embarking on this journey across the brutal Sonoran Desert, the only obstacle between starvation and the highly-alluring prospect of having two, maybe three meals a day and a pair of shoes without holes and maybe even, someday, a used Ford pickup and a three-bedroom condo. This is a journey only appealing to desperate people. But the majority of people in Mexico are desperate and the Perezes, who had never been able to earn enough for a daily mouthful of beans, were no exception. There were far too many farm laborers in Mexico and far too few fields. So Rosa offered her talents mending a pair of pants or a shirt here and there. Pablo had an occasional tourist agree to let him wax a car for 35 or 40 pesos – enough to buy two liters of milk and a loaf of bread at the corner market or 5 little tacos and a soda at the taco stand.

Rosa's mother, Conchita Herrera, had hired these particular coyotes because of their reputation. One of them had transported two of her sons without incident. Conchita, weeping and wiping her face on a white hanky, stuffed a stack of corn tortillas in Pablo's pack and kissed the three good-bye, saying over and over again, "que vayan con los angeles, que vayan con los angeles." *That you may travel with the angels.*

Conchita had no way of knowing that the coyotes she hired were not just nominal animals, but actual animals. They do what they please, to whomever they please, and on one dry hot June night, it pleased a couple of them to do it to Pablo's wife, while a third held Pablo at gunpoint just 200 yards away encircled by palo verdes and ironwood trees. In Pablo's arms, asleep under the star-dotted black desert sky and the threat of a bullet through her head, was his baby daughter. So Pablo made a decision, when that horror was all over, that his family would not be getting back in that van. Rosa wept violently and launched a bitter protest because she knew what that decision meant. Three of her cousins, who couldn't afford a coyote, had died of dehydration in this very desert. Rosa insisted that the damage had already been done, so they might as well at least get a ride out of it. Pablo was convinced any man who would point a gun at the head of a sleeping two-year-old is far more dangerous than the desert.

"We have to take our chances, Rosa," he held firm. "We cannot stay with these monsters."

"What about water?" she asked. "We don't have nearly enough."

"We have enough," Pablo told her. "We'll hitch a ride by the time the sun comes back up again. You'll see, my love. Everything will be alright."

The morning light proved Pablo's plan wanting. The three motorists who had come their way over the course of the moonless night had just kept driving. And now the travelers were facing the unwelcome dawn, foreboding for the wicked heat it was sure to bring. The small puffs of dust rising from their footsteps were tinged pink by the rising sun as they trudged toward the distant mountains imprinted in dark purple on the pale blue horizon. The new, revised plan was to put one foot in front of the other, crossing into Arizona and traversing miles of wilderness territory through the second largest Indian reservation in the nation. The Tohono Oodham Indians revere those mountains as sacred, because, according to native legend, they are the place where life began. But on this day, the Baboquivari Mountains cast the threat of death in their shadows. Pablo had made a decision to part from the road in an effort to make a direct route to one of the few places unsecured by border barriers. He had done his research on how to enter on foot a while ago, before the coyotes became an option.

Pablo's tongue stuck to the roof of his mouth, as if he had been drinking glue. He had taken not more than two sips of water for himself. His mouth stuck to itself with each word he spoke. He spent his words trying to persuade Rosa to take water, but she refused, insisting on saving it for Carmen.

"Rosa, my love, you have to drink. If you don't make it, neither will Carmen. You've got to keep yourself hydrated." Rosa finally agreed to drink a couple of mouths full. Pablo had a red cotton bandana draped over Carmen's head as he carried her in his arms, his feet as heavy as anvils, growing ever heavier with each step, until finally at some point in the endless journey, a black curtain fell over his eyes and a high pitched tone filled his ears with a numbing pressure. The curtain lifted for a moment to reveal Rosa's contorted face floating before the backdrop of a serene blue sky. He became aware that gravel was cutting into his scalp on the back of his head. Then the curtain fell again and all that was left for his senses was the faint and furious wailing of his baby girl.

He awoke in a clinic. A nurse, who spoke perfect Spanish, explained to him that a band of Indian youths, looking for a place to drink a case of beer, were flagged down by a young man dressed in black clerics, standing in the middle of the remote dirt road. The priest led them on foot a short way off to find Pablo lying nearly dead. He helped the Indians load Pablo into their beat up Chevy truck and waved them on, refusing their offer of a ride. When they looked in their rear view mirror, they saw nothing but dust from their own vehicle. The stranger had vanished.

"Rosa and Carmen!" Pablo shot up in bed, and the plastic line passing life from a hanging bottle into the needle in his vein swaggered with the sudden shock. "Where are my wife and daughter?"

"I'm sorry, Mr. Perez," the nurse said, pressing gently on his shoulders until his head stiffly hit the pillow. "It was too late for them. They were already deceased."

"How?" Pablo shot up again. "How can this be?"

"They died of dehydration Mr. Perez. I'm very sorry."

"How can this be?" he sobbed. "How can this be?"

"I'm sorry," said the nurse. "I'm so sorry."

Pablo was treated for heat stroke and dehydration for three more days, at which time the nurse told him he was strong enough to be discharged.

"Mr. Perez, would you like me to help arrange for you to go home?"

"No." His eyes were locked into a vacant stare. "There's no such thing. I'm going to California."

# 5

## A Preference for Gold

Uncle Jimmy and Aunt Georgia flew in from Denver for the weekend to say goodbye to Lily and to Pablo. They probably wouldn't see either of them again. They brought two of their grandchildren with them. The kids were very excited to be staying with their Aunt Terry. Mom and Dad have a house that loves kids. It has a large yard with a trampoline, tire swing and a tree house. Its basement is stocked with toys for every age group, including an ample amount of the latest electronic entertainment for the older set. It is a place where the doorbell rarely rings, because the regulars know to let themselves in, and the only thing that stands between a new friend and the fun that lies within is a screen door through which someone from inside will holler at you to come on in. Although Mom is an interior designer, she has forfeited the more fashionable yellow and white striped sateen loveseats for reclining couches upholstered with scrubbable microfiber and equipped with their own drink holders. It is not a fancy, but a warm home, alluring for its comfort and its contents, which includes a stocked refrigerator and someone older and wiser than you who is genuinely interested in how your day was.

Mom brought Jimmy over, after situating Georgia and the kids at her house. Jimmy hugged Lily and went down on both knees at her bedside.

"How are you doing, little sister?" he asked, wiping her hair from her face. "You always had the most beautiful hair. Remember when we were kids, you used to let me comb it? No one else, just me."

Jimmy talked to Lily about childhood for a good half hour. Lily stared into space.

"In some ways, I imagine, raising Lily was actually easier than raising us," Mom said, lost in the memories of childhood that Jimmy had conjured up.

"I know that's a true statement where I'm concerned," Jimmy said.

"Remember that time in the hotel room?" Mom said. "You and me were just bouncing off the walls. Auntie Bev and Uncle Jack were just about at the end of their ropes. I know if it wouldn't have resulted in loud wails, Auntie Bev would have taken us by the scruff of the necks and knocked our two heads together Three Stooges style."

"Yeah, and then amidst all the chaos, someone asked, 'Where's Lily?' because no one had seen or heard from her in well over a half hour. And it turns out she had found the magnifying mirror in the hotel bathroom and had entertained herself quietly making faces in that thing."

"And Auntie Bev says to us 'Why can't you two be more like Lily?'"

"And at that very moment, Lily stuck her fingers in her lips and stretched them out as wide as they would go and looked into the mirror, and we looked over her shoulder and told her she looked like some Wallace and Gromit character. And Lily was so offended, she screamed at us, and Auntie Bev decided not to take us out to dinner that night."

"Yeah, we ate those orange crackers with peanut butter in the middle and granola bars from Auntie Bev's purse and went to bed."

"The next day, we left Lily alone with her mirror."

"Hey," Mom said, bolting out of her seat. "I wonder." She left the room and returned with the hand mirror from my bathroom. She held it in front of Lily's blank face. We all adjusted our positions so we could see Lily's reaction. There was none. Mom slowly put the mirror down on the side table. After that, Uncle Jimmy spoke *about* Lily instead of *to* her.

"Do you think she knows I'm here?" he asked me later as we all sat watching the Winter Olympics.

"I don't know," I said. "Sometimes I think she knows more than we think she does. But there's no way of knowing."

"I feel like I let her down, Beth," he said. "Everyone thought it would be me who watched over Lily all her life. But where have I been? I missed it all."

"Well, you knew she was well taken care of. If she had needed you, you would have been there."

"You have no idea how close we were as children," he said, arms crossed, watching a Canadian skier glide over the moguls.

"I still remember watching this event as a kid. With Lily. One of the skiers said he was dedicating his run to his brother, who had Down Syndrome. The guy was a long shot to win, but he ended up pulling it off. I remember looking at Auntie Bev and saying that if I ever made it to the Olympics and won a medal, I was going to give it to Lily."

"That's sweet."

"Yeah, well, Lily was my buddy. I still remember, we were watching the Olympic figure skating together and Auntie Bev asked her if she wanted to do that someday. She said, 'Yeah, with Jimmy.' Made me kind of feel sorry for her for a minute that she would never be able to figure skate. Until I remembered that I wouldn't either."

"I know she thinks the world of you, Uncle Jimmy," I said.

"Mom has told me how much she looked up to you. From what I hear, it wasn't always easy to get Lily to do the things she was supposed to, but somehow, you always could."

"Yeah, Auntie Bev used to call the power I had over her 'Jimmy magic.' For some reason, I would just ask her nicely and she would respond to me like she wouldn't respond to anyone else."

"I still think you were promising her French Fries when the rest of us weren't in ear shot," Mom said.

"She and I just had an understanding," said Uncle Jimmy.

"Well, it's probably because you played with her a lot." Mom said.

"Sometimes, she was my only ally," Jimmy said. "When I went through my annoying phase and no one else could stand me."

"A phase? Exactly when did that end?" Mom asked.

"Watch it."

"Uncle Jimmy?" I said.

"Um-hmmm." He took his eyes off the TV and looked at me now.

"If there's any chance that Jimmy magic could still work, could you ask her to come back to us?"

Lily is the only one who, I am certain, would treat me the same exact way no matter what I told her about me. She doesn't have it within her to see any evil in someone she loves.

"I really need her, Uncle Jimmy."

He smiled. "I'll give it a try. Why don't you get some sleep. I'll sit up with Lily for a while, tuck her in and go on back to your Mom's. I'll bring Georgia back with me in the morning. She'll love to catch up with you."

"OK." I kissed Uncle Jimmy on the top of the head. "See you in the morning."

Before I drifted off to sleep, I thought of Lily and an old yellow dog that had come into the shelter. Lily had quickly grown attached to Murphy and asked if she could bring him home. I agreed to it because she so rarely asked and it was such a sweet old dog. Something about his eyes, looking straight into yours with an astute and uncharacteristic insight into the human condition. About three months after Murphy came to us, we discovered he had tumors and likely wouldn't survive a surgery. His condition deteriorated quickly. He was in agony and I thought it best to put him down. When I told Lily, she begged me not to. Lily understood euthanasia. She had seen it before at the shelter. It was on several occasions that she held the head of a dog in her lap, sinking her chubby hand into his fur, pressing her forehead against his until the moment the injection did its work. But Murphy was a different story. He was not a generic companion animal. He had become a friend to Lily. I wished I didn't have to make this decision to take her friend away. But I didn't want to see Murphy suffer any more. Early before Lily woke up, I loaded him into the back seat and headed to the shelter. Lily had said her good-byes the night before and went to bed, sniffling and wiping her eyes, without looking at me. As I drove, I heard the poor animal's faint whimper with each heavy exhale. I couldn't get Lily's tear-streaked face out of my mind. "Dear God," I prayed, "Why do I have to make decisions like this?"

I pulled into the parking lot, taking the speed bumps slower than usual, so as not to jar Murphy into any additional suffering. I got out, reached into the back seat and hoisted him up. As I did, he let out a final trembling snort and I felt him go limp and heavy. It was beautiful. I was able to go home and tell Lily that Murphy died in my arms, all on his own, at the time appointed to him.

ಬ⚹ಞ⚹ಬ⚹ಞ⚹ಬ⚹ಞ⚹ಬ⚹ಞ⚹ಬ⚹ಞ

I served Aunt Georgia some espresso and biscotti at the kitchen table. Jimmy and Pablo were watching Olympic commentary in the family room with Lily.

"How are the kids doing, Aunt Georgia?" I asked, passing her the sugar and a demitasse spoon.

"Good. We just found out our baby is going to be a Rhodes Scholar."

"A Rhodes Scholar? Annabel is a Rhodes Scholar? I've never known one of those before.

"Me neither." Her thick lashes fluttered as the steam from her espresso rose up over her eyes.

"That casts our family in a whole new light, doesn't it?"

"I suppose so," she said, smiling broadly. "You should see the list of Rhodes Scholars and all their accomplishments. Politicians, writers, professors, scientists. It's quite an impressive group."

"Where will she be going to school?"

"The College of All Souls of the Faithful Departed of Oxford in England."

"Wow."

"I know, Beth. It almost seems like a fairy tale. The college was founded in the 1400s by the king and the archbishop of Canterbury." She dunked her biscotti into her espresso, took a bite and laid it back down on her saucer. "The scholarship pays for everything, thank goodness. Room and board and two years post graduate study."

"That's amazing," I said. "A Rhodes Scholar in our family. Well, one thing's for sure. She must have gotten her brains from your side of the family. From what I understand, Uncle Jimmy does not have a stellar intellect. "

"Oh, well, people underestimate your Uncle Jimmy, Beth. They always have. But I don't know where Annabel got her intelligence. None of us are brilliant like she is. I mean we can all function, but Annabel functions on a whole nother level."

"She's a genius, huh?"

Georgia looked out past me, far away.

"When Annabel was born, I looked into her face and I said to myself, 'This child I hold is not an ordinary child. She will not have an ordinary life.' Don't ask me how I knew that, but I knew it. So, I'm waiting to see what it means."

"It has to mean something," I said. "I mean, a Rhodes Scholar. That's quite unusual. What are there, like 50 of those a year worldwide?"

"Fifty two. But that's not what the 'not ordinary' thing meant. There's more to it. Much more."

I smiled and looked at the paper clip Georgia was working to unbend.

"What is it?"

"I don't know yet," she said. "But I know her life has a profound purpose. She almost didn't make it into the world. Do you know that the doctors told me before she was born that she would have Down Syndrome?"

"Really? Why did they think that?"

"That's what the amnio said. It happens occasionally that you get a false positive on those things."

"That's scary," I said. "Don't' some people choose to terminate based on those results?"

"Most do," Georgia said, pensively. "We very nearly did."

"You did?"

"I know that's probably shocking. But it's a very scary place to be. And you're thinking about the best thing for everyone involved, especially the child. How much the disability will cause the child to suffer. You're weighing it all and just trying to do the right thing."

"Yeah."

"Yup. If it weren't for Auntie Bev, Annabel probably wouldn't be here."

"Really? Auntie Bev talked you into going through with the pregnancy?"

"No. She didn't talk me into anything. She just told me the truth."

"Which was?"

"Many things."

She pressed her fingers on the Biscotti crumbs left on her saucer. "But if I had to sum it up? In one word?"

"OK, sure."

"Life."

"Life."

"Yup. Life. Imperfect, unpredictable, messy life. Loving people who have imperfections is part of it. A big part of it."

"Yes. We all have imperfections."

"Right. I came very close to not having Annabel because we thought she had Down Syndrome. But I can guarantee you this. I wouldn't have loved her any less if she hadn't been a Rhodes

Scholar. Or if she hadn't been named MVP of her softball team. Or if she never even learned to walk or write her name. Annabel is mine, and I couldn't have loved her any more or any less."

"That's beautiful."

"That's what I learned from almost having a child with Down Syndrome. Imagine what I could have learned from actually having one."

I smiled. "I have learned so much from Lily."

"I wish I could have been around her more. But you know Jimmy. His job has been so demanding and he doesn't like to travel at all."

I nodded.

"But I really do wish. I wish I could have known Lily better."

"Maybe there will still be a chance," I said.

"Oh, I hope so, Beth. Is there a possibility?"

"The doctors say no. But we can still hope."

"Yes, we can always hope."

"I just find it very difficult to believe there is going to be a world without her. Pablo too. It's just so hard to picture them gone."

"Not gone," Georgia said. "Just elsewhere."

We drank more espresso, looking at our cups between sips.

"You know, for three nights in a row, right before her stroke, Lily had a number of very realistic dreams about Auntie Bev. One morning she told me Auntie Bev came to her in her sleep and sat on the edge of her bed. When Lily reached out for her, she disappeared. Lily said she started crying, and Auntie Bev reappeared, standing at the foot of her bed. 'Don't cry,' she told Lily. 'I'll see you soon.' Then she disappeared. The following night Lily had a dream that she was a little girl again, sitting in Auntie Bev's lap as she read a book to her. After she was done, she closed the book and Lily asked to read another one. Auntie Bev told her she didn't see too good without her reading glasses, but suggested they pray a Rosary instead. So Lily was a little perplexed, because, she said, Auntie Bev never wore glasses.

She asked me why Auntie Bev would need glasses in Heaven. I didn't know the answer to that one."

"That's a tough one," Georgia agreed.

"And then the next night, Lily dreamed that Auntie Bev came and sat on her bed again. 'I want to tell you something important,' she said to Lily. 'I spoke to Agnes tonight and she told me that Terry's rosary used to be silver.' Lily told her she preferred gold. And Auntie Bev told her, 'Then keep praying.' And then she vanished."

When I told Danny about this, he said this had happened to his and his mother's rosaries on a pilgrimage to Medjugorje. He had worked as a fisherman one summer during college and earned enough money to fulfill his mother's lifelong dream of seeing the place where the Virgin Mary appeared to a group of young Balkan visionaries in Bosnia.

Danny said rosaries turning to gold are a somewhat common experience among those seeking holiness through praying the Rosary. All of a sudden, they notice the links connecting the beads have turned from a silver to a gold tone.

As he was telling me this, it dawned on me what a different childhood Danny and I had. He was raised by a struggling single mother who cherished her son and the ideal of family love. His father had walked out, so his mother redoubled her efforts to engulf Danny in happiness and surround him with all things good. As a result, Danny grew up with faith and hope. I had little faith from the start and had lost whatever I had of hope by the time I hit puberty. I don't know exactly why, but I do know that it was around that time that I came to understand the lack of affection between Mom and Dad. There wasn't anything overtly wrong – no arguing or tension. There was just an air of stale blandness in our home that I found profoundly dissatisfying. I ached for depth, any kind of depth at all. Even if that depth meant deep wounds. I wish I had been raised by the same couple who brought up my baby brother John. Something dramatically changed between Mom and Dad when John came along. You could detect it with your five senses. The home was imbued with a certain new glow and it wasn't just because Mom had redecorated with splashes of Latin American color. There was a re-institution of breakfast, and we were often awakened by the smell of comfort wafting from the griddle. We took turns reading to each other at the table – from books like Shakespeare, which none of us understood, but we enjoyed because of the music of the words. Later in the day, there came the frequent screeches of the screen door followed by the footsteps of friends, showing up for slow-baked family dinners, which had made the microwave obsolete for virtually all things but popcorn. On cold days, we were wrapped in the warmth of pajamas made of red and green plaid flannel, which Mom had ordered for every member of the family to wear on Christmas Eve. Late-night laughter often flowed like a sonata from my parents' bedroom as they lay in the dark together. These are the things you notice when you grow up in a house where two people love each other.

These are the things I imagined Pablo grew up with. Pablo learned how to make tamales from his grandmother, Lita they called her. All the women would gather the day before Christmas to make them, usually a quantity of more than 300, to be shared among the families of all present from Christmas to New Year's Day. The large undertaking was financed by Lita's tamale fund. Every time she went to the market, she would come home and drop her spare change into a tin coffee can, which she kept in the cabinet over the stove. By December, there was enough in the can to buy the ingredients for the tamale feast. This was one of the few times of the year when the Perezes would have meat.

All women present would be put to work chopping and shredding, stirring and wrapping. But Lita allowed only two sets of hands in the masa – hers and Pablo's. Anyone else might spoil it. Pablo was never sure how he merited such an honor, but he thought maybe it was because he was the only male interested in the goings on of the kitchen and he had participated in the culinary rituals of both tamales and menudo since he was 4 years old. And hadn't once ruined the masa.

"Lita always said that food had to be prepared with love," Pablo said. "If you prepare food when you are angry or upset, it will not taste good. I will tell you, there was enough love in that kitchen to make the most delicious meals you have ever eaten in your life. I can still taste it. Every time I smell the chiles, I feel my grandmother's arms around me. That is what tamales are about, Mija. Tamales are about the love of your family. And that is why I want to share this with all of you. I will try as best as I can to remember how Lita taught me."

This is what he told the gathering of non-Hispanic women – four whites and an African American – who gathered in my kitchen to make a traditional Mexican holiday dish ten months too soon.

Pablo assigned each of us a job. Mom was to boil and blend the chiles. Katie was to soak and dry the corn husks. Georgia was in charge of shredding the beef. Laura and I were to chop all the ingredients for the salsa that would accompany the Tamales. Pablo would, of course, take care of the masa.

"And Lily, you are the kitchen guardian," he said, planting a kiss on her forehead, as she sat propped in her bed just outside the kitchen door. "You are to supervise and bless the whole production with your love and beauty."

This put my mind somewhat at ease. I had been a little worried about the one thing Pablo's grandmother considered vital to the making of a good tamale, but I was fairly certain that Lily had more than enough love to drown out the flavor of any animosity the rest of us may hold toward each other.

Laura and I have never been best of friends, and I worried that some bad feelings might percolate between us and permeate the food. As much as I enjoy spicy dishes, I wasn't sure how tasty the tamales would be if they were tainted by our red hot tempers. Best to leave the heat to the anchos and jalapenos.

I don't know if it was the fear of spoiling the tamales or Pablo's positive influence, but Laura and I were on our best behavior. You might even say we bordered on amiable. Laura inquired as to the welfare of the animals at the shelter, and I asked what each of her children were involved in. We stood side by side, passing our knives swiftly through the vegetables, glancing from time to time over at Pablo's hands, deep in masa, the lard rising up his wrists.

"We never really cooked together when we were kids," Katie said, carefully flattening a soppy wet husk onto a towel. "Why is that, Mom?"

"I don't know," Mom said. "I guess by the time you were old enough to be useful in the kitchen, I was afraid to have you all in the same room with so many sharp implements that can so easily be used as weapons."

"We're doing OK now," I said, chopping.

"Yeah," Laura said. "Beth and I are even standing next to each other, with knives in our hands, and there hasn't been one drop of bloodshed."

"Why didn't you girls ever get along?" Katie asked. "You're both such nice people. I could never figure that out."

"Aside from the fact that she robbed me blind and never had a kind word to say to me, she was a great sister," Laura said.

"That was when I was very young," I said. "But she never got over it. She never could just move on."

"Well, we're moving on now, sister dear, because we have twelve dozen tamales counting on our mutual adoration," Laura said, "Right Pablo?"

"You must at least put up a good front," Pablo winked. "Trick them into thinking you love each other."

"Speaking of mutual adoration," Katie said, "how is Danny? Have you seen him lately?"

"He's fine," I said. "We're just giving each other a little space right now."

"Oh, Beth," Laura said, "I was sure he was going to be the one. Not only is he gorgeous and sweet, but you can almost see the chemistry between you two. Seeing you two together takes me back to when Paul and I were dating. I remember the days were so long, waiting to get off work and see each other. New love is wonderfully torturous, isn't it?

"And then you marry them and it's a whole new kind of torture," Mom said, smiling and chopping.

"Oh, you and Dad are so cute together, Mom," Katie said. "You can tell you are still crazy about each other after all these years. I hope it will be that way for me and Gary."

"Actually, you know, it can get better and better," Mom said. "Only if."

"Only if what?" Georgia asked.

"Only if you live your married life in accordance with that famous Kennedy quote."

"The Kennedy quote?"

"You mean 'It's an unfortunate fact that you can secure peace only by preparing for war?'"

"No, not that one."

"The one unchangeable certainty is that nothing is unchangeable or certain?"

"No."

"Those who foolishly seek power by riding on the back of a tiger ends up inside?"

"No."

"Life is not fair?"

"No, no. Now, if you'll all be quiet I'll tell you: 'Ask not what your marriage can do for you, but what you can do for your marriage.'"

"I have a priest friend back home," Pablo said, scraping the masa off his left hand with his right. "He is ninety-something years old. He has married close to a thousand couples. Every time, he tells them the same thing. He tells the bride and groom, 'Did you think you came here for a wedding? No. You came for a funeral. For your own funeral. In marriage, you must die to yourself.'"

I had many questions about that. But I only asked this: "Are we ready to wrap the tamales?"

# 6

## *Children of Eve*

The results of Pablo's CT scan were not surprising, but I fought back tears anyway.

"I don't understand, Pablo," I said, driving him back from the doctor. "I don't understand why you have cancer. And why your family had to die. And why Lily is lying there comatose in a bed in the middle of my family room."

"You mean, Mijita, why is life full of suffering?"

I sniffed and nodded, wiping my nose and eyes on my sleeve.

"Ah, an age-old question," he said, handing me his hanky. "I, like you, used to ask questions like that in my youth. I spent so much time asking that question that I finally came up with an answer and I haven't had to ask it since."

"An answer?"

"Oh, you would like to know it?"

"Sure. Wouldn't everybody?"

"Ah, yes. But you are one fortunate enough to know a wise old man, such as myself." He grinned, and I sniffed and managed a smile.

"I have spent most of my life, Beth, wondering why my life was spared and the lives of my beloved were not. I am tormented by this. All my life, I am tormented. And I may never know the answer to that. But this, I do know. Every human tragedy is the result of a decision made by somebody, somewhere. Think of the Blessed Virgin. She could have said no to God and Jesus would not have been born. What if she had said no? We would have all been lost. No incarnation. No cross. No redemption. No salvation. But she said yes. So salvation came into the world through her. The rest of us will never have a question that important to answer. But we have many others. How many of us say no to God, all of our lives and what do all those no's add up to? Why do I have cancer? Maybe God tried to send us a scientist to cure cancer, and that scientist's mother said no to carrying that child, and with that split-second decision to terminate a pregnancy, all the course of human history was changed."

"So you have to suffer for her decision? That's not exactly fair."

"I have said my own "no's" to God. And someone else suffers harm from those. No man is blameless in contributing to human suffering, unless he has said yes to God in every question. There are only two people I know like that. One is the Son of God and the other the mother. And they only have that kind of a track record because both of them were born with the benefit of being unstained by original sin. The rest of us, we are sons and daughters of Eve. We are still feeling the effects of the fall of our first parents. They said no to God and we will suffer forever more, until the lion lies down with the lamb."

"So how do you explain earthquakes? Those cannot be the fault of humans."

"Maybe not. But, here again, God must do what He must do to get our attention. When I was a little boy, I was always getting into some kind of trouble. And every time I did, my mother would give me extra chores to do. My baby sister looked up to me and tried to grow up as fast as me. She wanted to be treated just like me. So one day, she asked Mama why she too was not given extra chores to do when she did something wrong. My mother told her it's because she did not need to be punished. She did nothing wrong. But, me, I was a hard head and had to be disciplined. It was the only thing that got my attention. And my sister would be upset because I couldn't play with her because I had all these extra chores. So whose fault was that? My sister did nothing wrong, but she lost a playmate. Was my mother to blame? Should she have let me continue doing bad things, or was she right to punish me, to try to change me? God must discipline the hard heads, not for the sake of his own revenge, but for the sake of the hard heads."

I nodded.

"Or maybe," he said, raising his index finger, "the one person who could have invented a way to prevent earthquakes starved to death in a third-world nation because someone refused to part with their excess."

"You have a brilliant mind, Pablo."

"My theory makes sense to you, Mija?"

"Yeah," I said smiling at him. "You are a wise man."

He chuckled. "Maybe my theory will turn out to be true. Or maybe it's just the crazy musings of an old lunatic. I imagine I will find out soon."

"Do you think you can communicate with people from Heaven?"

"Sure, if they're listening."

"Will you try, Pablo? I will miss you terribly."

"Of course, I will, Mija. But you know, I'm probably going to be in purgatory for quite some time. So if you don't hear from me right away, it's because I'm temporarily tied up. Say prayers for my soul, Mijita. That is the greatest gift you can give a loved one. My soul is in great need of prayers."

"OK, Pablo."

"Just think of me and say this, Mijita, say: 'May the souls of the faithful departed, through the mercy of God, rest in peace.'"

"I will long for these moments we have together right now, Pablo. I'm so glad our paths crossed."

"And they will again someday, Mija." He kissed me on the forehead. "We will see each other again in Heaven. In a place where there are no more tears. Only love and laughter and joy. I will introduce you to Rosa and Carmen and Jen. You will really like them, Mijita. You will really like them. And you will tell me that I was right about everything I said about them."

I shook my head and smiled.

"You don't believe the things I have told you? You will see, Mija. Someday, you will see."

"How did your faith survive such great losses as you have had?"

"It didn't. I had to rebuild. I abandoned my faith for many years after my wife and baby daughter died. At first, I placed all the blame on God. Then later, I realized that I felt responsible for their deaths and unworthy of God's love."

"But you only wanted the best for them. You tried to protect them."

"Yes, only the best. But I was a proud man. No one was going to do what those animals did to my wife again, while I stood by helpless. I knew deep down what Rosa said was true – that we did not have enough water. I made her go out in the desert anyway, with our precious little daughter. That is foolishness."

"You didn't know how it was going to turn out, Pablo."

"No. No one can see the future. It is only for God to see. But a fool indulges his pride at any cost, regardless of what the future holds."

"God could have saved them. He saved you, didn't He? Why didn't He save them?"

"That's what I couldn't figure out either. That's why I blamed Him for so many years. One day I realized I was thinking like so many Jews in the days of Jesus. They were waiting for a political Messiah, someone to save them from persecution and oppression under the heavy hands of the Romans. Jesus was not that. He was a savior of souls, not a savior of flesh. Yes, he heals and makes miracles, but only for the benefit of souls, so we can come to believe. So God did save my wife and child. He saved them from this world. But why not me? I couldn't figure out why. But now that I have lived my life, I know. He had a lot more work to do on me. He was not finished with me yet."

ᛒᏱᏣᏱᛒᏱᏣᏱᛒᏱᏣᏱᛒᏱᏣ

I have made up my mind not to see Danny again. Now I just need to tell him. I feel a profound sadness at my decision, but I know it is right and just. The last time he called, I told him that I was discerning the future of our relationship. He had a most surprising response.

"I'll pray for your healing, Beth."

The part about praying was what I found odd. Although I know he does pray because I have witnessed it myself, I had never heard him talk about praying. I rarely did it or talked about it, although I never have thought it was a bad idea.

I decided writing Danny a letter would be best. There was so much ground I wanted to be sure to cover and a verbal explanation left too much room for omissions. I hand wrote the letter in blue ink on plain white paper.

*"Dear Danny,*

*"I never thought I'd tell another human being what I'm about to tell you, Danny, but I'm going to tell you because I know it won't make a difference between us. Now that I know all hope is gone for us beyond friendship, there is nothing for me to lose by telling you. I'm going to tell you because I think it will be good for you to know why it could never work between us. I want to make sure you know it has nothing to do with you. I'm also going to tell you because you're safe. I actually need to tell someone. No one in my life knows where I've been or what I've done. I can't stand the isolation any more. I'm hoping that if I reveal the secret, it will lose its power over me.*

*I hope you don't mind, I'm going to give you the long version.*

*When I was 14, my best friend's older sister invited us to come along with her to a party. A 19-year-old named Brian was there. He gave me a free sample of the drug he was dealing in exchange for my virginity. I guess he thought it was an even trade, considering the drug was "ecstasy." He provided some for me and then I provided some for him. This was the arrangement we kept for the next several months, until one night, he got mad at me because I was late, slapped me across the face and called me a whore. He accused me of having been with someone else. I had been. I had fallen for a senior named Travis Gold. I was beginning to learn from Travis that love provides a high even better than drugs. So I no longer needed Brian. He never had a chance to slap me again.*

*In one way, Travis was good for me. He never did illegal drugs. He said it was too risky. His father was a cop. He wanted to be one too and didn't want a juvenile record. I cleaned up my look in order to keep him. I instinctively knew he was drawn to glamour girls, not trashy drug addicts. Sex had initially drawn him in, but I knew it wouldn't hold him for long. I wanted him for long.*

*Shortly before my family moved to Seattle, Travis broke it off. He had turned 18 and now our relationship was suddenly illegal. He couldn't take a chance on getting in trouble with the law for having sex with a minor. That's what he said, anyway. I actually think he couldn't bear to look at me anymore after what had happened between us the month before."*

My hand struggled against writing the next sentence. I was relieved by Pablo's knocking. He wanted to know if I cared to play a round of Canasta with him and Jimmy. I gladly left the letter in my upper drawer to finish later. While I shuffled cards, Pablo asked me how I had come to set up the animal shelter. I welcomed the chance to retell a happy event.

"It was actually a romance that launched my veterinary career," I said, dealing. "Not my own romance, but my sister's."

Laura found a stray one day and took it home. She posted pictures of the scrawny Italian greyhound in a one-mile radius from where she had found him darting in and out of traffic.

Three days later, she got a call from a man whose gardener had left the gate open. The dog had wandered more than twenty miles from home. His owner happened to see the posters while he was on his way to the airport to pick up his girlfriend. He gratefully offered to pay Laura a reward – or at least something to cover the cost of feeding his dog while the animal was in her care. She refused to take anything. As he left, she felt profoundly sad that the gentlest soul she had ever met just passed right through her life, without exchange of e-mails or phone numbers.

About a week later, on a Saturday morning, her doorbell rang. She opened the door to a toothy young man holding the leash of a panting Italian greyhound in one hand and a bouquet of white daisies in the other.

"I hope you don't mind me coming by unannounced," he said, "but I don't have your phone number. Here, these are for you. I just wanted to say thanks again."

He said it all in one breath, as if he had rehearsed it a number of times and needed to speak quickly to remember his lines.

"Thank you, they're lovely," she said. "But, really, there's no thanks necessary."

"I thought maybe I could take you to breakfast."

"What would your girlfriend say about that?" she asked.

"Well, she probably wouldn't be too happy," he said.

"And that doesn't bother you?"

"Anything good between us super-nova-ed out a while ago," he said. "We're just so many light years apart, we haven't seen the explosion yet."

"I don't know exactly what that means," she said. "But I'll have breakfast with you anyway."

Two years later, when Laura and Paul sent out wedding invitations, they asked for donations to the animal shelter in lieu of gifts. The best man led the procession into the reception hall, flanked by maid of honor, Katie Lovely, and Spinet, the Italian greyhound whose wanderlust had launched two people's common eternities.

Since I had no money to donate to the animal shelter, my wedding gift to Laura and Paul was a one-year commitment to volunteer at the shelter. Before the year was up, I had enrolled in Seattle Central Community College in pursuit of an eventual veterinary science degree at University of Washington.

"That is what I always wanted to do," Pablo said, "ever since I rescued a poor wounded stray from the train tracks in Guaymas. Isn't it odd that you ended up living my dream. We have a very close connection, you and me."

I smiled.

"So tell me, Jimmy," Pablo said, wrapping his small, boney hands around the double deck of cards. "What was it like growing up with Lily?"

"It was always interesting," said Jimmy, raising his arms straight over his head and stretching from the waist up.

"I'll bet it was," said Pablo, shuffling.

"It could be somewhat of a challenge," Jimmy said. "But there were also some benefits to having Lily as a sister."

"Like what?" Pablo asked, dealing.

A broad smile grew across Jimmy's face. He told the story of Connor, the punk bully in fifth grade. Bragged about smoking and the things he had supposedly done with girls, although nobody could imagine any girl desperate enough. This kid was not what you might call good looking. He was always doing things for shock value, like lighting matches in the school restroom. He called Jimmy stupid because Jimmy wasn't impressed. Jimmy always tried to ignore him. He was pretty good at it, too, until one day after school, when Connor's cruelty turned in Lily's direction. Connor advised Lily to learn how to talk if she wanted to avoid being made fun of the rest of her life. No one likes a retard, he told Lily, except maybe the retard's brother. He shoved his face into Jimmy's, twisted it into ugly contortions and said, "your face looks like crap." Where Jimmy got the self control, remains a mystery to this day, because the urge to hurt Connor very badly was overwhelming. And Jimmy knew he could. Even though Connor was 11, almost 12, and Jimmy had just turned 10, Jimmy towered over Connor by a head. Not only did he have body mass in his favor, Jimmy had civility and the conviction of all that is just and fair on his side. Anyway, Jimmy just grabbed Connor's shirt and said, "Watch it" and something incoherent about Lily being a much better person than he is. Connor scuffed away blabbering something about diminished mental capacities.

The next time Jimmy, Mom and Lily had any contact with Connor was at a carnival. Nobody knows why Connor picked those three kids to follow and harass when he had a whole fairground of kids to choose from. Maybe there was a comfort level there. He felt at home with his loathing for Lily and her siblings. He had no way of knowing he was about to become Lily's project.

First, she endeavored to win him over by hiding behind carnival booths, jumping out at him and saying, "boo," with a smile that pressed deep dimples into her big, round cheeks. Conner scowled at her, unmoved.

Then, she followed him as he hung his head and paced endlessly and aimlessly, back and forth across a short footbridge that lead across a wash from the games to the rides. Mom and her friend from school, who were playing in the wash not far below, kept an eye on them. Jimmy had gone off with one of his friends from the neighborhood to ride the Himalaya. Lily just kept following Conner back and forth across that bridge. He turned his head a number of times to look back at her. Each time, she smiled coyly, said "hi," and waved. He ignored her and walked on until he got bored enough with that activity to sit on a rock under a tree on the ride side of the bridge, elbows propped on his knees, which were poking out through the holes in his jeans. He threw an occasional rock into the wash, but missed Mom and her friend, each time.

Lily stood silent before Connor, waiting. He looked up at her with hostile eyes. Lily took his hand, pulled on it and said, "here."

"I'm not going to come with you, retard," he told her. "Go find your moron brother."

"Hey," Mom called up at Connor. "Knock it off with the nasty names."

"You," Lily said, pointing first at Connor and then at herself and then to the ferris wheel.

"Thanks for the offer, retard, but I don't have any more tickets." He stood up and pulled the inside of his pockets out. "See? You're just wasting your time."

Lily reached into the plastic purple Hello Kitty purse hanging on her arm, pulled out a strand of tickets, ripped them in two and held the largest half out to Conner.

The two locked eyes and stared each other down, Lily with a grin and Conner with his usual glare. Finally, Conner reached out his hand and swiped the tickets. "OK, let's go," he said. "But when these tickets are gone, you better leave me alone. You got it?"

"Yeah," she said, smiling.

"Oh, Lily," Mom called up. "Don't give him your tickets. He's not our friend."

While Conner and Lily rode the ferris wheel, the Crazy Wave and the Gravitron, Jimmy and Mom had reunited and were discussing Lily's strange choice of companions. She had always been a pretty good judge of character. So how could she have gotten it so wrong that night?

"Maybe she thinks he's unhappy and she's trying to cheer him up," Mom suggested, as she and Jimmy stood waiting for Lily at the funhouse, one of the few things at the fair that required only one ticket.

Since Lily had run out of tickets and Connor was left with two, amazingly enough, that's what he had decided to spend them on. She and Connor came out together. Lily smiled and grabbed his hand. He pulled it away and walked quickly to get ahead of her. Lily rushed to catch up and grabbed his hand again. This time, he kept it. He walked with her until Lily saw Jimmy and ran to hug him.

"I've got to go now," Connor said to Jimmy. "Here's your sister back."

Lily ran after Connor as he left and grabbed his hand again. "Tha," she said.

Conner looked back at Jimmy.

"Means thank you," Jimmy said.

Connor shrugged. "You're welcome."

After that day, Connor never harassed Lily or her siblings again. But there came a day when a third grader decided he would take a crack at belittling Lily for her lack of intelligence.

"Hey," Connor said, standing at an uncomfortably close distance to the twerp. "Back off. She's got more brains than you ever will, you moron."

Connor turned Lily around at the shoulders and escorted her away. Lily looked back and waved at the kid who had teased her. "Bye," she called.

Connor pretty much insured that no one at Jefferson Elementary School would ever mess with Lily again. Or Mom or Uncle Jimmy either. It must have been a comfort to have an enlightened bully in your corner.

# 7

## Guaranteed Cake

Jimmy promised Lily to try to come and see her again. With the possible exception of Lily, we all knew it was unlikely. Jimmy looked lost when he hugged her good-bye. It was a sadness like I've never seen on him before. Lily just blinked.

"Don't forget me, Lily, OK? Don't forget. Will you smile for me, Lily? Just one little smile? Remember the magic, Lily. Just one little smile."

Lily blinked again.

Not long after Jimmy and Georgia's departure, the next visitor arrived. John decided to come home for spring break. He wanted to spend time with Lily and help out with the animals.

Of all of us kids, John was the closest to Lily. She was a second mother to him. John is the true baby of the family. The next youngest child, Katie, was almost 12 when he was born. I don't know if it's because of Lily's influence or if John would have been John even if he was raised by wolves, but he is a tender soul.

Before he went off to college, John and I had a custom of getting together once a month, ever since he was eight years old and I moved out on my own. He was the only one of all the siblings left at home and I wanted him to feel a part of us, even though he didn't grow up with us. One night, when he was about

59

14, he confided in me that there was something he was ashamed of and he needed to tell someone. I had noticed he hadn't been himself. He had started hanging out with a few boys who seemed like trouble – the ones that can never look you in the eye and refuse to respond with more than a grunt when you address them.

It was a dreary sort of night, rainy and cold, so we decided to stay in and watch a movie. I made clam chowder and corn bread.

The steam rose before John's face as he broke his muffin apart. He swallowed hard before he put a bite into his mouth. He stared into his chowder as if a sad picture was afloat in there.

"I'm just so stupid," he said.

"Uh-oh. What did you do now?"

"Something really stupid."

"Well, it can't be any stupider than all the stupid things I did when I was your age."

John just stared into his soup.

"Try your chowder."

He twisted his mouth to the side and took a sip.

"It's good," he said, without expression.

"Thanks," I said, taking a sip. "So, what'd you do?"

"A couple of my friends – well I don't know if I should call them that – but, they were making fun of Lily."

"And you decked 'em."

"No," he said. "I wish I had. I joined in."

"Oh," I said. "In front of Aunt Lily?"

"No."

"Well, just don't do it again. And you may want to think about losing those friends. Or teaching them a lesson. In a charitable, not too painful way, of course."

"The things they said were so horrible," John said, shaking his head. "I mean, I feel bad because I was ashamed of Lily. I've never been ashamed of her before. She's never given us any reason to be."

"No. She is a wonderful person. If you have to be ashamed of a sister, be ashamed of Laura."

John smiled. "Or you."

Laura and I have clashed all of our lives. Two girls, so close in age, so far in perception and ideology.

It's been particularly tense between us ever since my niece Debbie's ninth birthday party. My parents do birthday parties right. Which is probably why everyone chooses to have their birthday celebration at Grandma's and Grandpa's. For Debbie's big nine, Dad rented a deluxe inflatable bouncer shaped like a pink fairytale castle, with a larger-than-life, three dimensional unicorn head above the door, poised like an elk head in a hunting lodge. In attendance were Debbie's three siblings, 14 cousins from both sides of her family, a slew of aunts and uncles, about two-thirds of the Maple Tree Elementary third grade class and several of Mom and Dad's foster children, past and present. So why it mattered that I had to leave early, I'm still not certain. I'm not even a favorite aunt. And I doubt, even if Julie took roll before the birthday song, that she would care that I was missing. But Laura had to make it an issue.

"You're never around for this family," she said. "It's like you have an allergy or something."

"I don't have an allergy. I have a cell phone. Which happened to ring and alert me that I need to go pick up a wounded animal. I didn't plan for that to happen during Debbie's birthday party."

"I'll try to explain it to her," she said.

"Laura, look around," I said. "She's not going to even know I'm not here."

"I don't think you know how much my kids look up to you, Beth," she said. "You paint, you take care of animals. You're gorgeous and you dress hip."

"Oh, please. Only you, Laura, could simultaneously flog and flatter someone. Come on. I'll make it up to Debbie. You know I will. I'll take her out for a Happy Meal next week. And bring her over to the shelter."

"Everything has to be on your terms, Beth. You've always been that way. Why can't you go along with what the family does? Mom and Dad hardly ever see you."

"So now I'm neglectful of my parents. Unlike you, of course, the perfect daughter, who is able to roll out grandchild after grandchild to occupy their time. Large quantities of their time, I might add."

"Are you jealous of that, Beth? Is that what this is about?"

"I'm not jealous, Laura, but you've always tried to one-up me. You know you have." I understood as I said it that my argument was growing ever more preposterous, to the point that even I could not determine a path that would redeem its integrity.

"Yes. You have discovered my evil scheme, Beth. I'm pushing babies out to make you look bad. You'd understand how ridiculous that is if you had kids. Single people have no idea how difficult it is to raise children."

"If it's too difficult, maybe you should slow down on the child bearing." I knew as soon as it came out, that was a big mistake. In our family, you can call each other rotten names, you can accuse each other of exploitation, you could probably even get away with inflicting a bad Indian burn. But you most certainly do not condemn people for having children. Children are highly prized gifts from God. "I mean, if you're overwhelmed –"

"I don't think my fertility is any of your business. And I'm not overwhelmed. This is what motherhood is all about – daily struggles and self-sacrifice, doing the things that are best for your children, even when you don't want to. That's what I'm doing, the best I know how. Maybe not exactly to your approval, but then, my happiness has never hinged on your approval. And speaking of that which brings us happiness, don't you have a sick animal to attend to?"

"Yes, I do," I said. "And you have a birthday to celebrate. So, let's not waste any more of each other's time." I slammed the car door hard and backed as quickly as I could down the driveway. Unfortunately, I don't think I was able to muster enough

which was nearly dislocated when I pulled the car door shut so hard.

I took my phone out of my purse and called one of my volunteers, who was happy to fill in for me. I sat there in the car for about fifteen minutes, trying to beat down my pride, which obnoxiously hounded me with the unpleasant truth that my sister had won this one. As a matter of fact, she pretty much wins them all.

When I returned to the party, Debbie, oblivious to my going and coming, had just blown out the nine candles on her birthday cake. I got there just in time to join in the cheering.

"What did you wish for?" asked a little girl with freckles and a missing tooth.

"Don't tell!" cautioned another little girl, this one with wildly curly hair, tied up in two bunches on either side of her head. "Your wish won't come true."

"Oh, it will come true," Debbie said, confidently. "It will absolutely, positively come true."

"How can you be so sure?" the freckled girl asked. "I've never had a birthday cake wish come true."

"Me neither," Debbie said. "Until today. But I figured it out now. I figured out how to make birthday cake wishes come true."

Laura cut the cake and gave the first piece to Debbie. A very large smile spread across the girl's face as she dug her fork into the pink frosting rose.

"How?" the curly-headed friend demanded.

"Tell us," said the freckled girl.

"Tell us what you wished for," said Debbie's 7-year-old sister Julie.

Debbie forced her words around the ill-mannered amount of cake and frosting in her mouth, so that her long-awaited response was muffled by the artificially colored, sugar-laced hydrogenated poly-unsaturated fat that had clung to her wide smile. "I wished for a piece of cake," she said.

## 8

# A Ban on Wheels

Mom took Pablo out to dinner, providing me with the first quiet moment I've had by myself in quite some time. The shelter had been a bear. It's difficult to comprehend how so many people can abandon their four-legged companions, but animal homelessness seemed to have reached near epidemic proportions. I really missed Lily's help. She was by far the best employee I've had. Not only did she truly love the animals, she was very methodical about all her duties. She never played favorites. There were some dogs that were objectively more handsome than the others, but you couldn't have proved it by Lily. She gave everyone the same ear scratch, followed by the chin rub and the back pat.

I brewed myself a shot of espresso and pulled the half finished letter to Danny out of my desk drawer. I took it to the family room, where I could keep Lily company while I wrote.

*"As I said, Travis was drawn to beauty. But now there was deliberate death between us and there's no way to make something beautiful of that. I mourned for weeks for Travis. I wished I had his baby within me still. Maybe that would have made Travis stay, but even if not, I would have still had a part of him inside of me and, eventually, in my arms.*

*Nothing I said could bring Travis back to me. So I went back to drugs. But now, instead of getting them for free from Brian, I had to pay for them. I did whatever I could to scrape up the money, including stealing from purses and wallets in my own home. I cared not one bit about the consequences of such betrayal. If I couldn't have Travis or his baby, I was not interested in having any other relationship with any other human being.*

*After the abortion, I realized that what I wanted more than anything else in life had no possibility of ever happening. I had wanted Travis to take me into his arms and love me and our baby within me. I knew he was capable of that. But he wouldn't do it. Instead, he drove. The consummate gentleman. Opened the car door for me. Brought me to his house to recover, so my parents wouldn't know that we had killed their grandchild. Drove me home later that evening. Walked me to the door. Told my parents I was feeling ill, probably from something I had eaten.*

*Travis' parents financed the procedure, quickly and quietly, so a new generation wouldn't prematurely materialize and spoil their son's future. In the final analysis, I was not good enough to bear Travis' child or his name. He would find someone else for such an important role. It wasn't to be me. This understanding that what I longed for would never be, this belief that a more worthy lover could have merited Travis' affections and saved a life -- these were the realizations that drove my attempts to anesthetize a chronic, gnawing ache.*

*I settled on speed as the anesthesia of choice. I would be still using to this day -- or dead – if we hadn't moved to Seattle to help Aunt Lily. Ask anyone in my family and they will tell you it was Lily who saved my life. Ask them and they will tell you that I was a good kid who got on the wrong track for awhile but went on to recover and make a success of my life. They will tell you that because they don't know better. I guess it all depends on what you mean by success. I am accomplished and I am clean. But my life has been one sad day after the next. I have a profound loneliness that I have attempted to fill with the compa-*

*ny of animals and an occasional boyfriend. I have a deep reali-*
*zation that this is not how my life was supposed to turn out. I*
*was supposed to have a soul mate and some children. I was sup-*
*posed to live out the life my mother and sisters have --*
*surrounded and whole. I am in a stark place, on a cold peri-*
*phery, outside looking in, nose pressed against the warm glow of*
*true fulfillment.*

*There are people in my life who would tell me it doesn't*
*have to be this way. Shortly after we moved to Seattle, a priest*
*friend of Lily's came for her birthday. It didn't take him long to*
*read the pain in my soul, and he made it his mission over the*
*next two decades to help alleviate it. This he did by trying to*
*convince me that there is such a thing as new beginnings be-*
*cause, and only because, God can forgive anything. I've known*
*this must be true, but I never could figure out how, so I've just*
*kept it in the back of my mind, simmering. Father Fitz had made*
*it clear that he had not only the Catechism of the Catholic*
*Church to back him up on this, but his own personal experience.*
*He himself had once made a fatal mistake. It was not difficult for*
*me to understand how God could forgive a teenage boy for driv-*
*ing drunk and accidentally killing his best friend on prom night.*
*He, after all, didn't mean to kill anybody. But I had meant to end*
*a life. Not just anybody's life, but that of my own flesh and*
*blood. I was certain God could never love anyone so despicable.*
*And if God couldn't, certainly no man could -- unless I kept that*
*part of myself secret, and I knew myself well enough to know I*
*could never keep anything so big hidden from someone I had*
*promised to share my life with. I also knew, even if I could find a*
*man to love me, I would have to deprive him of children. I am*
*certain that I am not worthy to ever be a mother. A mother pro-*
*tects her child. She does not kill it. And of this, I am still firmly*
*convinced. I do not have motherhood in my future.*

*So this is why we can't be together. I am truly sorry, Danny.*
*I wish you all the best in finding true love.*

*Always Your Friend,*
*Beth*

I felt a satisfaction at having written the letter well. It said exactly what I wanted to say. It explained everything accurately.

"I'm going to send this letter tomorrow," I told Lily, folding it in thirds and pressing the creases firm between my index finger and thumb. "Unless I lose my nerve."

I took *The Far Side* off the shelf and read a bit of it to Lily. It was the first time I had picked up the book since Lily's stroke. Lily and I always had a bedtime ritual. Pajamas, face, teeth and then a half-hour of sitting together on the couch, leafing pages, giggling and reading out loud from the coffee table book full of cartoonist Gary Larson's best stuff. None of it really seemed funny without Lily's laughter.

The phone rang and it was John. I put him on speaker so he could tell Lily all about the exams he has coming up, the professor with a Mohawk, the terrible food served at the union and the cute girl he went to a movie with Friday. The amazing thing about John is his ability to hold down a conversation all by himself. Most women and all old people can do that, but young men typically aren't any good at it.

John has always been such a nice kid. He didn't inflict all the typical teenage misconduct on his family. His rebellion -- if you could even call it that -- peaked on the day he came home with the serenity prayer tattooed on his forearm. Mom and Dad broke out into hysterical laughter when they realized there was a typo in his tattoo.

"Lord grant me the serenity to *except* the things I cannot change, the courage to change the things I can and the wisdom to know the difference."

"Well, son," Dad said, "This would be a good time to put that prayer into practice cuz that tattoo is one thing you can't change."

John looked embarrassed and worried.

"Well, I think it a nice tattoo," Lily said, rubbing the words on John's arm. "I wan' one too."

"Just make sure you go to a tattoo artist who has spell check," Dad told her, chuckling.

John did not laugh.

"Oh, don't worry, Honey," Mom said. "Ninety-nine out of a hundred people will never even notice. People are so illiterate these days."

"Yeah, and if you ever find yourself applying for a job as a proof reader or a copy editor, you can always wear a long sleeved shirt," I said.

"Honey, whatever possessed you to get a tattoo anyway?" Mom asked. "You know you're stuck with that thing for life."

"It's a good witness," John said.

"Couldn't you just wear your faith on your sleeve, like everybody else in this house?" Dad said.

John was such an adorable little boy. Every night, right around midnight, he'd wake up, and climb into someone's bed. About once a week, it would be mine. He'd bring with him his tattered blanket with the blue baseballs and his plush toy he called Short Elephant. It was green with an originally purple tail, which was more of a brownish tone since it had been so often sucked on and squeezed. I don't know if John has ever gotten over the fact that he lost Short Elephant one day while running errands with Mom. After calling every store and place of business on the route that day, Mom had to break it to John that his loyal old pachydermic pal was not coming back. Dad had gotten it on a business trip to Denver, and Mom was never able to find another one, even after hours of surfing online toy stores.

I regret that, even though I was the oldest child, I wasn't much help to Mom when John was a baby. I didn't want to look too closely at him for fear that I might see myself in his genetic makeup and begin to agonize over a loss that can never be recovered.

But as he grew to be a toddler, I started to see him as his own little person, rather than another drop in the family gene pool. The most endearing thing about John was his shortness in relation to the volume of hair that he had. It always looked like he would fall over from top-heaviness. I miss that little frame of his, which would fit so perfectly in your lap – all of it, including curled-up legs and arms and wadded up blanket tucked in close.

There are so many things I wish I could have back. I wish I could have Lily's laugh back. Especially the one she used for things that no one else would ever notice, much less find funny. I would, at times, hear hysterical giggles coming from behind the bathroom door. Outside the bathroom, Pablo Puppy would be sitting with his back against the door. The first few times I witnessed this, I could not figure out what Lily was finding so funny in there. I finally decided to ask.

"Come 'ere," Lily said, pulling me into the bathroom and shutting the door.

"What is it?" I asked.

"Jus' wait," she said, staring at the door, bending forward, hands on her knees, eyes and mouth wide open in joyful anticipation.

Before long, there appeared a long skinny tail, beneath the bathroom door. Lily touched the tail with her index finger and it moved from side to side in an off-beat rhythm, sending Lily into hysterics. She would compose herself long enough to touch it again to reactivate the awkward wag.

When I think of life with Lily, these are the kinds of things that come to mind. Though, if I think harder, I realize there were more important things.

If it wasn't for her, John probably would have never been born. And if it wasn't for her, he would have already died. I'm sure Lily saved John's life on more than one occasion, but one particular moment comes to mind. She saved his life on a day when his dying – anyone's dying – could have gone completely unnoticed, masked by the revelry of family, friends and food that is the Thanksgiving holiday. It was a day when so much happiness filled the house and spilled out into the backyard, that no one would have noticed a Lego jeep wheel had entered the mouth of a 4-year-old boy, who was supposed to have passed the stage when toys with choking hazards were forbidden. But jeep wheels end up even in the mouths of older children, who realize

70

that teeth are far more efficient than fingernails for taking things apart.

Mom says if it wasn't for Lily, who paused the beater and left her chocolate chip cookie dough to go see what John was doing, the boy would have laid there in his room struggling for air until death overtook him. Mom tore up the stairs when she heard Lily's terrified screams and performed the Heimlich, expelling the small treaded wheel from John's windpipe. Lily cried for close to thirty minutes after it was all over. The tightness of her embrace made it difficult for him to resume his playing, but he found a way – without wheels on his Jeep, of course. Every plane, train or automobile that entered John's life from that day forward had to be enjoyed without wheels. Lily saw to it that they were all retrofitted for safety.

Maybe John turned out to be such a good boy because he never got away with anything, thanks to Lily's vigilance. If he left the room, she would let no more than thirty seconds elapse before going to track him down. This was partially because she was a mother hen. But even a mother hen casts her gaze away from her chicks at some point during the day, if only to scratch dinner for her little ones from the dusty ground. Lily's attentiveness was partially due, I'm sure, to her obsession with cuteness and her affinity for make believe. Whatever John played, Lily played along. They shared a world that the rest of us only watched from the sidelines. It was a happy world, but it was not utopia. A military was necessary to ensure peace. The two playmates spent a good part of their day supporting the efforts of partially clothed, but fully armed G.I. Joes, digging trenches in the flower garden and scouring the backyard for sticks to be used as blockades. Lily and John were the only ones among us who could make a gunshot noise convincing enough to freeze Timbledee Sniff stiff in his hamster wheel. Their impression of an exploding grenade was also superb, better even than Jake's.

ଔଞ୍ଚଔଞ୍ଚଔଞ୍ଚଔଞ୍ଚଔଞ୍ଚ

Laura was supposed to bring the kids over to see Lily and Pablo Thursday afternoon, but Mom called to say that Julie was going to the hospital for some tests. She was feeling nauseous, fatigued and irritable and Laura noticed a yellowish cast to her skin. Preliminary blood tests showed that Julie's liver function is compromised. I asked Mom if Laura needed any help with the other kids and Mom said she was taking care of everything.

"Please ask Lily to pray," Mom said. "She is so close to our Lord."

"OK," I said. "I will. Don't worry, Mom. Julie will be fine. Won't she?"

"Oh, I hope so, Honey. I am so worried, Beth. Oh, ask Pablo to pray too."

"I will."

"And you too, of course, Honey."

"Yes," I said. "But, Mom, don't worry so hard. We don't even know what the problem is yet."

"I know, Honey. You're right. It's just that Julie is like one of my own."

"I know, Mom."

When I hung up, I went to Lily's bedside. Pablo was still napping on the couch by her. I sat on Lily's bed and put my head on her chest. "Julie is sick, Lily. Will you pray for her? Mom wants you to pray for her."

I heard a faint grunt, deep in her chest. I looked into her face. She blinked blankly.

"Lily," I said. "Are you going to pray for Julie?" I watched for some sign that she understood. I got none.

"Tell me, Lily. Tell me if you are." I put my ear back on her chest. I heard nothing.

"Tell me, Lily. You can do it. You can tell me."

I wondered if I had imagined the grunt. I rewound the whole thing in my head and heard it all over again. No, I had not imagined it. I was sure I had not.

The day passed with no word on what might be wrong with Julie. Test results were due back in 24 hours.

The doorbell rang at close to 9 p.m. It was Danny.

"I got your letter," he said. "Can I come in?"

"Sure." I held the door open wide for him.

"My 7-year-old niece is in the hospital," I said. "She has something wrong with her liver."

"How serious is it?"

"They don't know yet. We should know more tomorrow. I thought I heard Lily grunt when I told her about it."

"You're kidding." He looked into her face, I want to say almost adoringly, as she slept.

"But she didn't respond again to anything I said after that."

"What, exactly, did you say to her to get a response."

"I asked her to pray for Julie."

"When did she fall asleep?"

"About an hour ago. Do you want to wake her?"

"No. I don't want to disturb her sleep. I'll come by tomorrow to see her. If that's OK."

He seemed suddenly self conscious, probably about having invited himself back into our lives.

"Where's Pablo?"

"He's over at Katie's for dinner. I see you got my letter."

He had been holding it in his hand. The paper had lost its crispness, like it had been read a number of times and repeatedly taken in and out of a pocket. "Yes," he said, contemplating it with his eyes. "Thank you for writing it. I know it wasn't easy."

"Well, to tell you the truth," I said, "I feel ridiculous now for having written it. I don't know what difference it makes."

He swooped me toward him with his strong arms and hugged me tight into his chest. "It makes a big difference," he said softly.

I loved being in his arms. "How?"

"Because now I know, Beth. Now I know you. So now we can go forward."

"Didn't you read the letter, Danny? There is no forward."

"There's always a forward."

"Not for us, Danny."

He released his grasp on me and took my hands in his. "Look Beth, you could let your past lock in your destiny. You could choose never to love again because you deem yourself unworthy. Or you could choose to make up for your past deficits. You could choose to love like you've never loved before, to a depth you've never loved before, by standards you've never lived by before. You could make your past mean something. For yourself and for someone else. You could put all that pain and instruction to good use, so it wasn't suffered in vain. Or—you could just choose to shut me out. Me and our children."

"Our children? See I think you missed the point, Danny. I am too screwed up to have children."

"Beth, you're forgetting what I do for a living. Most people haunted by their past have never come face to face with the ghosts that are rattling the chains. They wander through this world in fear, making decisions they believe are random, but are really connected to every other decision they have ever made. You have done all the work of identifying the source of your pain. You heard the rattling of the chains and went to investigate and discovered the demons. Now, what are you going to do? Just live with them?"

"They're not bad roommates," I said. "They never leave any dirty dishes in the sink."

"They will ultimately destroy you, Beth. In the end, it's you or them."

"Spoken like a true product of the video game generation."

"Do you want a life without love, Beth? Is that what you want your legacy to be? It's your choice, Beth. Choose the vast chasm of nothingness. Or choose redemption."

"So, it's that simple? I just will myself to be unburdened by my past."

"No. It won't be easy. It will take work. But I can help you, Beth. Please. Let me help you. I can do this. It's what I do, Beth."

"Nobody is that proficient," I said.

"Why'd you tell me, Beth?" The question sounded almost confrontational.

"What?"

"Why'd you tell me about all that stuff in your past? Why'd you write this letter." He held the folded paper in front of me and stared me down.

"I told you why," I said. "I told you because I thought you should know the reason I can't marry you. I thought I owed that much to you."

"You told me because you thought I could help you."

I didn't look at him. I just shook my head.

"Come on, Beth. You don't want to live like this. Let me help you."

I drew a heavy sigh. I was so attracted to him, he was nearly irresistible to me. "OK, doc," I said, with mild sarcasm. "It's all yours. Give it your best shot. I sure hope you're as good as you think you are."

"I'm even better. Just wait and see, lovely, Lovely lady. You have no idea how good I am."

&#8359;✂&#8360;

# 9

# *Disney Rage*

The day after Julie was released from the hospital, with the diagnosis of liver failure with unknown cause, Pablo doubled over in pain with chest pain just after breakfast. The paramedics rushed him to Harborview Medical. Nurses punched his medical ID number into the central health system while he was en-route and accessed his entire medical history, learning that he is a terminal cancer patient. Pablo went into cardiac arrest in the emergency room. The E.R. doctor told Mom that he assumed the patient would not want to prolong the dying process.

"That's why so many terminally ill patients have 'Do Not Resuscitate' instructions -- for situations just like this one," he said.

"He doesn't have a DNR," Mom screamed at the doctor. "Plug him in!"

The doctor looked at the nurse, who shook her head, apparently to confirm that the patient indeed lacked the legal document necessary to relieve the doctors of their ordinary duty to try to preserve life.

The doctor tried to talk sense into Mom by telling her that putting terminal patients on life support only needlessly prolongs their agony. It's hard for the families to see them go, but it's the most humane choice, he said, especially for a patient so elderly.

"It's not time for him to go yet, Doctor," Mom insisted in an elevated tone. "But If you don't try to save him, it will be time for you to call a malpractice attorney."

"Your decision, Mrs. Lovely," the doctor said calmly. "I can only imagine what you must be going through."

And with that, Pablo was given another shot at survival. Two weeks later, he was sitting in a wheelchair back at Lily's bedside, filling her in on the secrets of good dog breeding.

"Temperament is everything, Mija," he said. "You really want to propagate faithfulness and loyalty – in any breed. Don't you agree, Beth?"

"Absolutely," I said, fixing Lily's covers around her shoulders.

Pablo sat quietly satisfied, thinking, I imagined, of all the good dogs he's had in his life.

"As soon as I get out of this thing," he said patting the arms of his wheelchair, "I'm going to need to take a trip home."

"What for?" I asked.

"I need to pack some things up, settle a few things. And I'd like to see my dogs again."

"OK, Pablo," I said. "We'll go together."

He returned to peaceful silence, gazing at Lily.

"You know, Mija, there are so many things this old man wishes he'd seen. I wish I had seen Rome. I wish I had seen the sunset from a hot air balloon. I wish I had seen the Rams win the Super Bowl from the stands. But more than any of that stuff, Mija, I wish I had seen Jen and Lily together. To be able to witness your grandmother as a mother, that would have done my heart good. I'm sure she was a beautiful mother. Just like your mother. These things get passed down through the generations. Someday, if God grants you children, you too will be a beautiful mother."

Pablo shifted in his seat, as if he had just noticed that he had something bumpy in his back pocket. "Oh, listen to me go on and on. This old man, can sure talk your ear off, can't he, Mija?"

"I love to hear your voice, Pablo."

"You are so good to me, Beth. I love you, Mija."

I bent over him and gave him a hug. Then I sat down on the foot of Lily's bed. Pablo and I both sat watching her.

"Do you think she's in any pain?" I asked.

"She doesn't seem to be," Pablo said.

"How would we know?"

"Well, she looks pretty peaceful."

"She looks vacant," I said. "Maybe her facial muscles just wouldn't be able to show discomfort."

"I think they would."

"How do we know?"

Pablo slowly moved his trembling boney hand out and placed it on my shoulder, guiding it with great concentration, as if he were operating a forklift or some non-member of his body. "I guess we have no way of being 100 percent sure," he said. "But she appears to be OK."

I would much rather suffer the most excruciating pain myself than to think that Lily is in any discomfort, unable to tell someone or ask for help. What if the corner of the pillow is poking her in the back? Or her night gown is crumpled underneath her? The thought of someone suffering alone, inside their own skin, with no way of reporting it, is greatly disturbing.

"Pablo, have you ever done anything you are ashamed of. I mean really ashamed of?"

"Oh, I don't think there is a person alive who hasn't."

"No, I don't think everyone has."

"Well, I'll tell you mine, if you want to hear it."

"Sure, if you want to tell me. But please don't ask me to tell you mine."

"Deal," he said winking. "This is a freebie."

"OK," I said, smiling.

Pablo's face turned suddenly serious, and I became worried about what he might reveal. "When I got to California, I was an angry, bitter man for quite some time. I could not figure out how it was possible that I should have to go through life without my speed to match my ire. Driving in reverse has never been my forte.

As a matter of fact, the only traffic citation I have ever received in my entire life was for "unsafe backing." I ran into a car as I was pulling out of a parking spot, into a street. In my haste to find out what kind of damage I had done, I jumped out of the car without putting it in park. And there my car went again, as if once is not enough to run into a medical malpractice attorney's brand new orange Porsche Boxter.

Within the very same month, I backed into a very large sedan, which was parked next to me, slightly over the line into my space, at an angle opposite mine. I misjudged the space I had and ran into the fender. I pulled forward, in horror, and decided to try again. But I was so upset, I couldn't figure out how to get out of the space without running into the car again. So I left my car there and ran two miles home to get Dad. I was afraid he might use the incident as evidence that I was not mature enough to drive at the age of 17. Getting my license had been a reward for having cleaned up my act. But instead of making me feel like a fool, Dad made me believe that this sort of thing happens at least as often as people clean out their ear wax.

"You should see the kind of damage I did when I first got my license," he said. "People locked their cars in their garages until I turned 21."

He returned with me to the scene and got our car free from that parking space, just by pulling forward, pulling back, pulling forward and pulling back. I watched in amazement. I had a cool Dad. Some kids don't. But I did. Then he left a note for the owner of the car to call us to get the damage repaired. I lived in dread for several months, waiting for the phone to ring. It never did. Laura resented that. It seemed to her like I had an uncanny knack for escaping consequences. Like the universe granted me a cosmic pass on the "what goes around comes around" principle.

When I got out of sight of Mom's house and that ridiculously indulgent birthday party, I pulled over, put my head on the steering wheel and rubbed my shoulder, deep into the socket, wife and daughter. I hated this country. I hated the American dream. For me, it had turned into a nightmare. It robbed me of my family. But I tried to make a normal life. I got a job cleaning hotel rooms. It was a good job. The best I'd ever had. I hated the people that ran the hotel. I hated the guests because they had things I did not. Not the cars and fancy homes and nice clothes. I didn't hate them for those things. I hated them because they had families. They were doing all these fun things with their children. Going to amusement parks, to the beach, swimming. Some of them were sour and exhausted and I resented them for not appreciating what they had. Some were patient and grateful and I resented them for having a life so good that nothing had tarnished them yet. To be that happy, I concluded, they must have been pampered all their lives. Then one day, I was cleaning a hotel room and saw a Minnie Mouse toy standing on the desk. She had on a pink dress with white polka-dots and that large ridiculous red bow and red high heels she always wears. She had this huge smile on her face and was holding her white-gloved hands in the air. I picked her up and pressed the button on her legs and her skirt lit up and twirled. All of a sudden, something just snapped in me. I took the toy and hurled it across the room. It crashed into a wall and broke. The arm was hanging on by a wire and I tried to put it back together, but the plastic was cracked. It didn't spin anymore. I dumped it in the trash and hoped the family had collected so many meaningless souvenirs that they wouldn't miss that one. Later that night, I couldn't get to sleep as I thought of that poor little girl and how unhappy she would be to find her Minnie Mouse gone. That's when I realized I needed help. I was scared of the rage I had felt that had led me to destroy something a child loves."

"What did you do? To get help, I mean."

"Well, I couldn't afford a shrink, of course. I just made a resolution inside myself to get myself better. I spent a lot of time alone. If I had known how to pray, I guess you could say I prayed. But I didn't really talk to God. I talked to myself inside my head and just kept telling myself there's something more out there for me. I told myself that I can't give up and I can't let myself go crazy. There was some kind of inner strength. And as I look back on it now, I know it was the Holy Spirit trying to reach me. I was receiving grace. The prayers I've said in the later part of my life somehow got me through the beginning, maybe. I don't know. Maybe because God sees all of time in a single moment, not in a straight line like we do. What's that word that means whatever you do now applies to something that already happened?"

"Retroactive?"

"Yes. I was receiving retroactive grace."

"Well, time heals all wounds, they say."

"Oh, but that is not true. No." Pablo shook his head. "Time? It just passes. It does not heal. God heals."

It's true that time had not healed my wound. A great deal of time had not healed. I was pretty sure a great deal more wouldn't either. But as for God, I wasn't in any position to ask Him for any favors.

I thought about how Pablo would feel about me if he knew. He was forced to live his life without the child he cherished. And here, I had made a decision to kill mine. A human life, disregarded and discarded. As if human beings are disposable. I don't know if I can say I didn't know what I was doing. I wanted to believe that I was having a procedure to remove some unwanted cells, like a tumor or some other kind of growth. Everyone at the clinic made meticulous choices in wording so as not to traumatize the patients. Everything they said and every mannerism they donned confirmed what I wanted to believe – this was not yet a baby. A woman in a burgundy nurse's uniform pushed a piece of paper in front of me and apologized that she even had to bother me with it. She said it was just a matter of procedure and bad politics that I must sign it. The paper stated that it is impossible to know when a fetus begins to feel pain and that a woman must be offered anesthesia for the fetus. But she assured me there was no pain involved in pregnancies as early as mine, and that I didn't need to worry about administering any medications to the mass of newly-formed cells, but I would need to sign the paper acknowledging that I was advised about the possibility of its pain and the availability of pain medication. The wording of that wretched thing kept reverberating in my head. There was even a moment, lying on the table with my legs spread apart, when I wanted to yell at them to stop. But I couldn't find my voice. I kept thinking of how upset Travis would be if I emerged from this room still pregnant. I bit my lip and hoped the abortionist would hurry up and arrive at the point of no return, so the horror of making the decision would be in my past. At each moment, up until that final moment, I knew it was within my power to stop it all. And yet it somehow wasn't. I lay there hating what was about to happen between my own two legs, a private place unlike any other in all of nature, a sanctum designed with only one purpose -- to protect and sustain life. Nature would find it unthinkable that this gate would be flung open to those who want only to destroy that which is meant to be, at all costs, de-fended.

I had waited as long as I could to make this decision. I had been holding onto hope of a life with Travis. We obviously didn't intend to conceive. If we had abstained or if the condom hadn't broke, I wouldn't even be here right now. Therefore, I reasoned, this baby – or mass of cells, or whatever it is – was never meant to be.

All that careful self convincing meant absolutely nothing at all in the moment it was all over. I was engulfed with a lucid and resolute certainty the very instant they turned off that monstrous machine.

"My baby is gone," I said inside my head, as tears squeezed out past my eyelids and down into my ears.

If there had been some way to trade places – if ripping my-self to pieces would have made that tiny life whole again – I would have done it. Gladly.

The following year in health class, I learned about fetal de-velopment and that my instincts, although they had surfaced too late, had not failed me. The "mass of cells" that had been forcibly removed from its quiet sanctuary had a beating heart, brain waves, a nervous system and fingerprints.

If the clinic had glossed over those details, could they have lied to me about the fetus feeling pain, too? I kept replaying over and over in my mind, what it must feel like to be ripped apart, limb from limb.

After getting Pablo into bed and tucking Lily in, I closed my bedroom door and picked up the phone.

"Danny, I thought I could do this, but I can't. It just doesn't feel right. I just have never been able to –"

"What? "

"I don't know."

"Say it, Beth. Come on. It's OK. You're safe. Say it."

"I don't' want to hurt your feelings, Danny."

"I'm tough, Beth. And you made this call for a reason. There's something you feel the need to say."

"I don't know if I'll ever feel --"

"Feel what?"

"You know I'm very, very fond of you, Danny. But I don't know if I'll ever feel what I felt for Travis. With anyone else. I've never felt it since. And it's been two decades and a long string of men."

"I don't know exactly what that feeling was, Beth. But I do know that you and I, we have something special. The person who felt those feelings of so long ago was a person who hadn't been hurt so deeply yet, a person who had fewer walls. That's not who you are today, Beth. You have come through many things. I doubt you will ever feel anything quite like what you felt then. But that doesn't mean that what you feel right now is not real."

"Danny, the bottom line is, I just don't see myself as a wife and mother. I've lived too long envisioning myself as something else."

"OK, Beth. Let's just take kids out of the picture. Can you just be my wife?"

"No, I can't."

"Why not?"

"I can't deprive you of children."

"I will never find anyone like you again, Beth. If I don't marry you, I may never marry anyone. Either way, I won't have children. So I might as well have you."

"Danny, it's just that the vision of me married to you, it just seems like -- a vision. It just doesn't seem real."

"So, what is real? Spending the rest of your life torturing yourself for a decision you made when you were a child? Letting one day in a 14-year-old girl's life lock in her entire future? Come on, Beth. You're an intelligent woman. You can't possibly believe that that makes any sense."

"Danny, I know what will happen. I know that if I have a child, not a day will go by when I don't -- oh, never mind, Danny, I am just very tired. I'll call you in the morning."

"Do you want me to come over? I'll come right over."

"No, Danny. It's OK."

"So, not a day will go by when you what, Beth?"

"Danny, I really need to get to sleep. I'm fading fast." I yawned to illustrate my point.

"OK, I'll let you go in a second, Beth. But first, you were going to say something about what would happen if we had a child together."

"OK, Danny. Let me see if I can make you understand this. If I had a child, that child would just be a constant reminder of the one that I didn't bring into the world. I can't live with that constant reminder every minute of every day. I just can't do it."

"I see what you're saying, Beth."

"What you're asking me to do is to give our child the love that was due my first child, just because this one happens to have come along at a time that was convenient to me. That to me just doesn't seem right. Does it to you?"

"No. It's terribly wrong. The only thing that's ever right is love. And you failed at that once, Beth. And I failed. But now we have the chance to make it right. We have a second chance, here. I don't think you'd make the same decision today that you did back then, would you?"

I was busy blowing my nose.

"It's a fair question, Beth. Would you?"

"No." I wiped my nose and threw the tissue across the room.

"Then, it's time to go forward. With a new resolution. Into a new day."

"OK. So how do I do that? How do I look into the eyes of my newborn child and not think about the one who isn't here?"

"That may not be possible, Beth. But what is possible is to love that child in your arms like you've never loved anyone before.

And to make that your tribute to the one who isn't with you. I don't think you will ever forget, Beth, if that is what you're trying to do. You probably just need to accept that a part of you will always be missing."

The tears threatened to pour, and I had to put down the phone.

"Are you there, Beth?"

I picked the phone up and heard the volume of my voice elevate through the tears I was forcing back. "I don't want there to be a missing piece of me, Danny. I just --"

"Beth, we shouldn't be having this conversation on the phone. I'll be right over."

"No, Danny. Don't come. I am so tired. I just need to sleep. Actually, no. I hate sleep. I always have a horrible dream. Night after night, the same horrible dream."

"What is it Beth?"

I'm putting up lost dog posters in the pouring rain. The wet is soaking through my tattered coat to my shoulders and arms. The puddles lap at my ankles, like a rushing creek. My toes are so cold they've gone numb. I am barefoot. And under my coat, naked. I feel a hand on my shoulder, heavy and large. I turn around and it's a strange man, with features too shadowy and grey for me to see.

"I know where your lost baby is," he tells me.

"No, no," I say, "it's not a baby. It's a dog."

To verify, I hand him a poster. He looks at it, closes his eyes and nods his head. He hands the poster back to me. I begin to scream. Under the word "Lost" on the poster is a picture of a dismembered baby. I wake up crying, my heart pounding, and I'm drenched in cold sweat. I try to comfort myself. Tell myself it's just a nightmare. It isn't real. But the fact of the matter is, it's both.

# 10

## *Though She May Forget*

Whoever drove my rental car last wore Onyx. I hate Onyx. I used to love it, back when I loved Travis. He wore it all the time, and on one unseasonably warm day in June, he wore far too much. The sweet, nauseating scent expanded like a balloon, pushing up against the insides of his car, pressing against every square inch of vinyl and velour, pressing its tyrannical thumb against my gag reflexes.

"Can't you drive any faster?" I said.

"You're anxious to get this thing done, huh?" Travis observed, without taking his eyes from the road.

"I'm just not feeling very well. I think the driving is making me want to puke."

I looked out the window and tried to forget my nausea.

"It's only just a little farther," he said, squeezing my hand. "This whole nightmare will be over soon, Babe. Just try to relax."

"You know what? I'm really not feeling well, Travis. Maybe you should take me home."

"We can't do that, Beth. We can't miss the appointment. You know that."

"Really, Travis. I think I'm going to throw up."

"You'll be fine once you get there, Beth. I'm sure they have something they can give you to make your stomach feel better."

I laid my head back and closed my eyes. Travis locked his fingers into mine, driving with one hand on the wheel. "It's going to be OK, Beth. Don't worry. Hey, listen. I was going to save this as a surprise, but I think you need something to cheer you up. So I'm going to tell you now."

"What?" I didn't lift my head or open my eyes.

"I got tickets for Blue Jim. For this weekend."

My favorite band. "Oh, OK," I said, motionless. "That's great."

"If you're feeling up to going," he said. "If not, we'll stay in and watch a movie or something."

"We'll see, I guess."

Travis parked next to a dark grey compact car with a bumper sticker that read, "Every child a wanted child" and another one that said, "Visualize world peace."

I tried to figure out how abortion might bring about world peace. Maybe if people who don't want children abort them, there won't be any stressed out parents in the world, so they won't raise kids who want to go blow things up? Maybe fewer children being born into the world means people won't be competing and killing each other over food and land? Maybe the mothers of madmen, like Hitler, will abort and the world will be saved from evil dictators? Maybe women will pursue their careers instead of parenthood, and more women in powerful positions means a more peaceful world? This puzzle, this supposed connection between abortion and peace, is the distraction I employed to busy my mind while the roaring machine ripped a baby from the quiet solitude of my womb.

I never did go to that Blue Jim concert. I wasn't feeling up to it. Travis ended up going with his best friend Louis. I stayed home in a fetal position under my covers, wishing I were dead.

Though decades have passed since that day, if I weren't driving, I would have returned to that fetal position upon the first whiff of that noxious drugstore cologne. I had, unfortunately, decided against using public transit and now I was stuck with this foul-smelling rental car. I tried to turn my thoughts to the future, to what I had gotten in this car for in the first place.

I had on my best slacks – grey with brown tweed nubs – a brown sweater and pumps with three-inch heels. I wanted to predict what was going to happen. What the grandmother whom I've never met was going to say, what I was going to say, how I would respond to what she was going to say. I wanted to re-hearse it with myself so I wouldn't be blindsided. But I couldn't even make it up in my mind. There were probably over a million possibilities and I couldn't convince my imagination to conjure up even one. I couldn't even picture what she would look like. She would have my mother's features, only they would be eighteen years older than my mother's. Deeper crow's feet. Sharper cheek bones. Slightly larger nose and ear lobes. Looser jowls. I couldn't picture it. Not at all.

I couldn't imagine either what excuse she was going to give for leaving two small babies alone to cry themselves to sleep in a filthy apartment every night while she went out to get high. I de-cided not to have any preconceived notions at all. Maybe it was best that way. There would be no disappointments. No surprises.

It hadn't taken long for people finders to locate Jolene Myer. There was a trail of severance decrees and apartment leas-es and phone records. And police records. Parole violations, bench warrants, failures to appear in court, sentencing hearings. Up until she was in her mid-40s, these were the documents that chronicled her life.

I took it as a sign that maybe I was supposed to go visit her when I learned that her nursing home was just fifteen miles from Pablo's house. I had accompanied Pablo home to help him pack up and distribute his belongings. Pablo was growing weaker by the day and he sensed that there wouldn't be much more time to put things in order. So, off we flew to Burbank, while John took care of the shelter and Mom moved in to take care of Lily. I was disappointed I wouldn't get to spend any time with John on his spring break. But there were only a few more months until summer and then he would be home again.

The nursing home was larger than I had expected. And more industrial, with its large, boxy profile, six stories of grey rising into an equally grey sky. The clouds hung low as if they were gathering in to eavesdrop. Who could blame them?

When I told Jolene who I was, she wrinkled her forehead and stated, "Really. Therese's kid."

She said it as if she didn't believe me. I explained I was out here to help a friend pack up.

"What'd you make a detour to this dump for?"

"I wanted to meet you," I said.

"Well, I ain't got no money. If you're looking for an inheritance, I'll just be real honest about that."

"No, no," I said.

"What you see here is what I got. And it ain't much. I suppose if I had money, I might at least have a visitor on Christmas. Someone who might wanna be written into my will. But no, I ain't got a blasted thing to bequeath or a blasted soul to bequeath it to. "

"So did you never have any more children?"

"No. You got kids?"

"No."

We were both lying. She didn't give birth to any more children. She did have more. I don't know how I knew this. Maybe because she cast her eyes away for a split second when she answered. Maybe because she quickly turned the conversation to me. I wonder if she saw through me as I saw through her.

"I've never been married," I said.

I could hear that someone was cleaning the room next door. I assumed its resident had died and they were getting the room ready for the next one. They were using something that sounded like a vacuum, but I doubted there were carpets, so it must have been a floor polisher. That dull, mournful roar, mixed with the cold and determined smell of hospital disinfectant and impersonal expanse of aloof white floors, provoked a wave of nausea that hit me as if some foul gas had been released, expanding instantly throughout the facility, filling the air with the toxins of reticent memories. It was the same mournful roar I heard when I was fourteen years old, alone on that table with my feet in stirrups and my legs spread wide to welcome the insertion of a lethal machine engineered to suck out the remains of new life.

My abhorrence of vacuum cleaners cost me $16,000 plus six and five-eighths percent interest over fifteen years. As soon as I moved into my house, I took out a home improvement loan, had all the brand new Berber carpets ripped up and put in wood floors. This made it possible for me not to own a vacuum.

I swallowed down my nausea and tried to distract myself back into Jolene's presence by looking for some clues to her past on her dresser or walls. There was only a clock on the wall and nothing on the dresser but a philodendron, a rose-colored plastic water pitcher and a box of tissues in a nondescript white box with grey lettering.

"Were you ever married?" I asked.

"Three times. I had my heart broken more often than most people change the channel on their television. I had so many lovers, a new one would be in my bed before the next Netflix movie would be in my mailbox."

"Do you have any family still living? Sisters? Brothers?"

Rain began to patter at the window. A deep sadness passed over Jolene's face and then a vile, quiet rage crept into her eyes.

"I think we covered that. I haven't got nobody," she said. "I am all alone here. Ain't you been listenin'?"

I didn't know what to say, so I looked out the window. "Wow, the rain is really picking up."

"I haven't seen my sister since I was 14. And my brother – I think I was about 25 last I saw 'im."

"Do you miss them?"

"Who?"

"Your brother and sister."

"If you really wanna know the truth, Elizabeth, who I really miss is my dogs. I had some really good dogs all my life. That's who I really miss. And they won't let me have 'em in this hell hole. I had to let 'em go to a shelter."

"I run a shelter," I said. "I'm sure they found good homes for your dogs. What were their names?"

"There was Blue. He was a husky mix with one blue eye and one brown one. And there was Ginger. She was part shepherd and part chow."

I was struck by Jolene's lack of curiosity about Mom and Jimmy. How could she not want to know how life turned out for them? Was her heart completely devoid of any connection to them? She had to have remembered holding them, feeding them, dressing them – at least once in a while. She had to have had at least a few good moments with them. A few normal moments common to all mothers and their children. Could Jolene really have forgotten? As that question bounced around my mind, I remembered the scripture written on a pro-life pamphlet I found at the back of our parish church the day my niece Julie was baptized.

> *Can a mother forget the baby at her breast*
> *and have no compassion on the child she has borne?*
> *Though she may forget,*
> *I will not forget you!*
> *See, I have engraved you on the palms of my hands.*
> *---Isaiah 49:15-16*

Here was Biblical proof that it is actually possible for a woman to forget her child. For the life of me, I don't understand how.

"Do your brother and sister know where you are?" I asked Jolene, moving a heavy white curtain aside to reveal more of the rain-spattered window. I had risen from my seat and gone to the window, hoping to draw some kind of inspiration from the world outside this stagnant room, hoping the fresh light might somehow illuminate my mind to ask the right questions. Jolene may not have been curious about biological relations, but I certainly was. I felt a deep need to know Jolene's life, down to the very last detail.

"Are they still living?" I asked out the window. "Your brother and your sister?"

"Don't know."

I turned and looked at her. She looked small in her chair. Her taupe polyester-blend pants hung over her bent knee as if there was nothing but skeleton underneath.

"We weren't exactly the Cleavers," she said.

I returned my gaze to the outside world and watched a man three stories below help his elderly mother into the car , holding her steady from the back. He folded up her walker and took it around to the trunk.

Jolene cleared her throat, making a disturbing noise that sounded similar to how villains die in super hero movies. "When I was 14," she stopped to clear her throat again, "my father decided to keep my sister and return me and my brother to our mother, whose life was a wreck. My brother and I were taken away from her by the state and separated and I ended up in one awful foster home after another. People telling me I was nothin' but dirt. And there wasn't no reason for me not to believe 'em. I kept running away. Rather sleep in a gutter, than be crapped on by those kind of people. But the cops kept haulin' my hiney back."

"I don't understand. Why would your father keep your sister?"

"She didn't put up no fight. She was two years younger than me. She let 'im do whatever he pleased to her. Me, I kicked him in the nuts and bit his shoulder one too many times. My brother, course, had no breasts, so he wasn't no use to 'im."

My phone rang. It was Pablo. He wasn't feeling well and wanted me to know he was going to lie down and take a nap.

I said rushed good-byes to Jolene, who was not at all unhappy to see me go, and hurried home to find Pablo stretched out on the couch under an old tattered crazy quilt, eyes closed, mouth open. I knelt beside him and put my hand on his chest, relieved to feel it fall and rise.

I called Mom to ask her if I should try to wake him up or just let him sleep.

"Wake him up to see if he's conscious," she said. "And then let him go back to sleep. I'll wait on the line."

Pablo smiled, when he saw my face, and drifted back to sleep.

"He's OK," I said. "Mom, I went to see Jolene today."

"What?"

"Jolene."

"Why?"

"I wanted to meet her. To fill in some blanks. I was curious about my family history."

"I've told you everything, Beth. Your family history starts with Jen Eagan. She is your true grandmother. And Auntie Bev, of course."

"I wanted to see the what ifs."

"Well, what blanks were you able to fill in?"

"I don't know. But I think she and I have something in common."

"What?"

"Addiction. That can be hereditary, can't it? I mean, there is a certain personality type. That's what Danny said."

"So, did you see any of your personality traits in her?"

"I don't know. There's something there. Something under the surface. You should come meet her."

"I have no interest. It's not that I hold anything against her, Beth. It's just that she is a stranger. She is not my mother. Jen is my mother and Auntie Bev is my mother. The woman who gave birth to me did nothing to take care of me. As a matter of fact, she did quite the opposite."

"People change, Mom. She's an old lady. Probably living with regrets. She'd probably like to know that her daughter forgives her. Don't you want to help her leave this world in peace?"

"Is she lacking peace?"

"I'm sure she is."

"What makes you think so?"

"There's a haunting emptiness to her. It fills the entire room. It's depressing. And a little scary."

"Hmm. Cozy. Makes me want to run into her arms."

"Oh, Mom. You can handle it. You're strong as an ox."

"Speaking of big smelly animals, where's Beatrice? I didn't see her when I did my rounds."

"She has a home."

"Really? Who's the saint?"

"Biker dude."

"Maybe breathing exhaust fumes long enough kills your sense of smell."

"Maybe. He really likes her and seems completely unfazed by her halitosis."

I spent the following day discovering for the first time what it actually means to "get your affairs in order." I made all the calls for Pablo, so he wouldn't' have to explain over and over again to insurance companies, banks, lending institutions and landlords that he is dying.

The following day, I decided to go see Jolene one more time before Pablo and I head back to Seattle on Sunday. I knew I wouldn't likely have the chance again and I had a slew of new questions flurrying around in my brain. She seemed not displeased to see me again, although I have had warmer welcomes.

"Oh, you came back," she said in a monotone, using her arms to lift and reposition herself slightly in her wheelchair.

"I wanted to say good-bye before I go back to Seattle."

"Hmm."

"And I wanted to ask you something."

"So, ask." She wheeled over to her bedside table and grabbed a pack of cigarettes.

"They let you smoke here?"

"Is that your question?"

"No. Well, I guess it is now. One of them."

"Ain't got no matches," she said. "They let me pretend. So what's your other question?" She rushed the conversation along as if she had somewhere to go.

"Did you ever reconcile with your father?"

"Reconcile? Hell no. If there's such a thing as justice and such a place as Hell, that man is feeling the heat right now, let me tell ya."

Jolene tapped her pack of cigarettes on the arm of her wheelchair. "And it ain't nowhere near hot enough."

Fire flashed in her eyes, which were surrounded by accordions of yellowed skin. An emotion that was something like a cross between fear of an eminent danger and dread of an impending disaster swelled in my gut. I hadn't actually thought about Hell as a real place since I was a small child. I'm certainly no expert on theology, but I have sat through enough homilies to know that mercy extends only to those who extend it. Forgive us our trespasses *as* we forgive those who trespass against us.

"Have you ever tried to forgive your father?" I asked her. "I mean for your own peace of mind?"

"The things he did are unforgivable." She held an unlit cigarette to her lips and puffed. "You have no idea, Beth."

I wondered if Jolene understood that she had carried on the tradition of her father's cruelty – in an altered form. It might have gone on for generations to come if the chain had not been broken by my two adoptive grandmothers. Because of them, I was raised, not in perfection, but at least in love. Though not always a valiant woman, everything my mother did took into account the welfare of her children.

"Jolene," I paused for a moment to figure out how to ask this. "Are you at all curious about my mother and uncle?"

"Curious. Yeah, but it ain't in me to be nosy. I figure you'll tell me what you see fit to tell me."

"What do you want to know?"

Jolene looked down at the cigarette propped between her fingers for several seconds and then looked at me with a furrowed brow. There was a very deep vertical line permanently etched between her eyebrows.

"Do they hate me?"

"No."

"They oughta hate me."

"What if I told you that they forgive you?"

"Forgive? No. You have to understand someone to forgive 'em. There ain't no understandin' a parent who walks out on a kid. For the kid, there ain't no understandin' that."

"No, I suppose not. I don't know if they will ever understand that. But there are things inside each of us that no one else will ever understand. We are all alone inside our own skin. I don't know what it's like living inside yours and you don't know what it's like living inside mine. And yet, we all have to forgive. If we didn't, there'd be no such thing as relationships. They'd end just as quickly as they started."

"I wouldn't know anything about those. The closest thing I ever had to a long-term relationship was with my dogs. And a couple of stray cats I used to put out leftovers for or open a can of tuna ever once in a while. On the nights I'd forget because I was too wasted to get up off the ground, I guess they'd forgive me because they'd come back again the next night and rub against my legs like nothin' ever happened."

The nurse came and told us visiting hours were over. I leaned over Jolene's wheelchair and gave her a kiss on the top of the head. Her scalp smelled sour and salty. Jolene laid her hand on my arm – the first time she'd ever touched me. Her fingers were crooked and ice cold. She didn't say anything when I said good-bye, as if my affection toward her had stunned the speech out of her. I was on my way out the door when she finally got her voice back.

"Beth, if your Mom's somehow forgiven me, she'll come and see me."

I forced a smile. "Maybe."

# 11

## The Future Comes

The oncologist said Pablo was going downhill quickly. He was losing control over his left side and his speech was starting to slur. These, according to the doctor, were among the indicators that Pablo was entering his last days. Still, he remained sweet and peaceful, unlike many brain tumor patients, whose brain damage and treatments turn them into rage-filled victims, unrecognizable to their loved ones.

The day after his doctor visit -- six days after we got to Burbank -- Pablo grabbed his chest, doubled over and gasped for air. Within 45 minutes of arriving at the emergency room, he was in a coma. Mom flew out that night, leaving Lily in Katie's care. Doctors said it was unclear how long Pablo had to live, but that it was a matter of days and not weeks, and that he would not regain consciousness before he died. The tumor had gotten large enough to do significant brain damage and his heart was extremely weak. Mom put her arms around him and wept, knowing she would never hear his voice again.

Just before dawn, I took Mom to Pablo's place to get some rest. She marveled at all we had gotten done. Just about everything was packed in boxes, each one marked with the name of someone in our family. The names were all written in my handwriting, except for one. Pablo had written "Beth" in jiggly script on a box that was secured with three pieces of postage tape. He told me it was a surprise, and he didn't want me to open it until after he was gone.

Laura called Mom to tell her that Julie's liver numbers took another leap. We were all worried sick.

Late morning, Pablo's neighbor, Mrs. Ruiz, stopped by to see how he was doing. She was beside herself, she said, when she saw the ambulance. She dabbed at her eyes when she told us how Pablo had, on more than one occasion, unclogged one of her drains.

"Such a good man," she said, her bottom lip slightly protruding. "Such a good man. So much like my Alberto, God rest his soul."

"Do you know who has his dogs?" I asked. "He told me he wanted to see them, but we hadn't gotten a chance. Whoever it was had talked to Pablo last week and begged off because they were sick and didn't want Pablo, in his weakened health, to be exposed to the germs."

"I don't know," said Mrs. Ruiz. "Maybe Lucinda from the church. She is a kind soul who can't turn any animal away. And she was helping to take care of Pablo – getting him to his doctor's appointments, you know. Me, I don't drive, but Lucinda has a car. Or maybe Betty. She is an old friend of his. But I don't think she likes dogs. Or she's allergic or something. She was over one day when I stopped by and the dogs were put away in the bedroom."

I missed my animals, especially Bruce. I wanted him to lay his head in my lap as I talked to him about how my heart aches. I glanced outside at the dog run and pictured Pablo scratching a bull terrier's ears. I saw another one stretching for a lick at Pablo's wide smile, but Pablo was too experienced at avoiding such sloppy affections. The last thing I needed is any more dogs to take care of, but I longed to hold onto a part of Pablo. To love something he loved.

"Mrs. Ruiz, do you have Lucinda's phone number?"

Jolene looked at us with a wrinkled forehead, as if we were vaguely familiar, but suspicious.

"You remember me, Jolene? Beth."

"Oh, I remember you," she said, staring at Mom.

"This is my mother," I said. "Terry."

"You're Terry?"

"Yes," Mom said, not moving a muscle. "How are you, Jolene?"

"Come over and sit down," Jolene said, nodding her head toward a grey vinyl chair. "Sorry there's only one chair, Beth, but you'll have to let your mother have it."

Mom looked at me, and I motioned her over to the chair. Mom sat stiffly.

"So, what brings you here, Therese?"

"I'm helping a friend. He's dying of cancer."

"Sorry to hear it."

"Thank you."

"You are very polite, Therese. Whoever raised you, apparently did a nice job."

"Yes, they did."

Jolene turned her eyes toward the window. There couldn't have been anything to see, since we were on the third story, and she wasn't close enough to the pane to see down to the ground.

"You had a much better life than you would have had with me, I'm sure."

"Beth told me what a terrible childhood you had," Mom said.

"I've had a great number of foster kids who have been through similar things."

"Then you understand why I did what I did."

"No. I am a parent now, and I cannot imagine doing what you did. I can't understand it any more than you can understand what your father did to you."

"He is why things turned out like they did. My life was always a mess. Since the day I was born."

"And what about your father? What kind of mess was he born into? You expect me to understand you, but you will never understand him."

"I don't want to understand 'im."

"Who could understand that kind of evil?"

"So I guess I will die hating him and being hated by you."

"No. I don't hate you. To be honest, I don't feel anything for you."

"That doesn't surprise me none."

"What about you?"

Jolene looked at her blankly.

"Do you feel anything?" my mother asked.

"Ain't felt nothin' for nobody since the day I grew breasts," Jolene said, coldly. "But I am glad to know you are OK."

"I'm O.K. But you're not."

The two were locked in a silent stare, which was finally broken when Jolene looked at the window.

"You are going to die a bitter woman," Mom said. "Look at you. Death is at your door and you're still making excuses and reliving the horrors of your entire life. You can't change any of it. You can only change the future. And there's only one way you can do that."

"The future?" Jolene chuckled bitterly. "I got no future, Sweetheart. As you pointed out."

"The future comes, whether you're here to see it or not. It comes."

Jolene looked at Mom, hard and puzzled, maybe not so much perplexed at the meaning of her words, as at the fact that my mother dared -- and cared -- to say them.

Mom went over and stood towering over the frail, weak woman who had once given life to two human beings, but would die with no one to sustain hers. Mom stooped and held Jolene's shoulders, looking straight into her sickly eyes.

"Seek mercy."

Mom said it as a command, as if she had been granted some kind of authority over this virtual stranger.

"Oh, you talk so crazy, Therese," said Jolene, casting her eyes onto her own gnarled fingers fiddling with the hem of her powder-blue polyester skirt. "What's wrong with you?"

"Seek mercy," Mom commanded again.

Jolene looked back at Mom. Her eyes softened in the path of Mom's forceful gaze. The old woman looked down again at her boney hands, rubbing first one and then the other for what seemed like a good two minutes or more. "I'm sorry, Therese," she said, still rubbing. "I'm sorry for everything. Tell James, too. I'm sorry."

"I forgive you, Jolene."

An awkward embrace followed, then not more than twenty more words were exchanged before we left.

"That was the most incredible thing I have ever seen," I said to my mother when we got to the elevator.

"I forced that apology out of Jolene, not for me, but for her. I have never been in such a dark place than in her presence, Beth. It scared the heck out of me. I feared for her soul."

"Maybe you should have told her that. She doesn't have much longer."

Mom shook her head. "I wanted her to ask my forgiveness, not because she wants to save her own hide from the fires of hell, but for the welfare of someone besides herself."

Mom glanced over at me and relieved my worry with a small smile, the way she always does.

"I'm not afraid for her anymore," she said. "Maybe she can have a peaceful death now."

"Do you think she believes in anything beyond this?"

"She will when she gets there."

"How do you always know the right thing to say?" I asked.

"Oh, I don't," she said. "Far from it."

"You do. I mean, how did you come up with 'seek mercy?'"

"Honestly, Beth, I don't know."

"Just came to you."

"Just came out of me," she said. "Probably the Holy Spirit's words, not mine."

My mother's life dossier does not lack impressive deeds, but I have never been so impressed with her than I was that day. I have never seen her so strong as in that moment, when she stared down a bitter old lady, and, I imagine, launched a thousand demons into tantrums. This old woman, who had spent her life harming instead of loving, snatched in the final hour from the jaws of the devil by the one she had harmed instead of loved. And this cosmic feat accomplished with an economy of emotion and only two words, which my mother had probably never in her life used together before that moment.

"Seek mercy."

It was brilliant.

༚ৡৎৡ༚ৡৎৡ༚ৡৎৡ༚ৡৎৡ

The doorbell rang at 7 a.m. Mom and I were still in our pajamas. We had planned to have a quick shower, pour our coffee into travel mugs and head to the hospital. I opened the door to a short, stout Filipino woman, who wore her salt and pepper hair parted down the middle and pulled back into a low bun. She was flanked by two bull terriers on leashes, stretching their necks and pointing their noses into the doorway, aching to get in.

"Hello," the woman said. "I am Lucinda. You must be Pablo's granddaughter. Manuela tells me you were asking about Ben Hur and Badger. Well, here they are."

Lucinda unhooked the dogs' leashes and they romped around the house, sniffing through the family room, into the kitchen and then on to Pablo's bedroom, tearing back through the kitchen and jumping up on the back door, tails wagging and ears flopping in a frenzied mission.

"Look at that," Lucinda said, still standing in the front room.

"They are looking for Pablo. How is our dear, sweet Pablo?"

"Doctors aren't offering much hope," Mom said.

"Oh, no," she said, grabbing her head dramatically.

"Would you like to sit down?" I said. "Would you like some coffee?"

"No, I don't want to keep you. I'm sorry to come so early, but I have to work. Such a beautiful man," Lucinda said, shaking her head. "You have no idea how many ladies would have given their eye teeth to get him." She put her head in close to us and whispered, pointing over her shoulder. "Like Manuela Ruiz next door."

Mom and I looked at each other and smiled.

"And I know at least five others, including myself," she said, returning her voice to its normal volume. She chuckled at her own cleverness. "Some of them are even twenty years younger than he is. There probably isn't a widowed old lady in our parish that would have turned down his marriage proposal."

"He is special," I said.

"How is his Lily?" Lucinda asked, stooping to pet the dogs, who had made their way back to her feet.

"Still the same," I said.

"Oh, Pablo was always so proud of his Lily. He talked about her all the time. How she saved him from his loneliness. You know, growing old alone can get quite depressing."

"I'm sure," I said.

"And look, in his final days, he is surrounded by family," she said, taking my face in her hands. "It is such a blessing."

We all talked about what would be the best thing to do with Pablo's dogs. We decided Lily should have them, so Lucinda left them with us.

I couldn't wait for Lily to meet Badger and Ben Hur. They looked so much like Pablo Puppy, the dog he had given her for her 35th birthday on his surprise visit to Seattle. I hoped that seeing them could reach something deep in her brain that nothing else has been able to reach. But, then again, if Pablo himself hadn't been able to do that, I don't know why I thought his dogs would. One thing I've learned from having loved ones sick, hope doesn't have to be rational. In fact, many times, it can't be.

ఴ❧ℂ❧ఴ❧ℂ❧ఴ❧ℂ❧ఴ❧ℂ

They called us to the hospital on Monday morning to tell us Pablo would not make it another day. His organs had all shut down. Danny offered to stay with Lily. Everyone else arrived at Pablo's bedside by 3 p.m.

About half-past four, Pablo moved his hand within Mom's. He lifted it ever so slightly. He opened his eyes and began to recite all of our names, slowly and with great effort. Then he closed his eyes again. Auntie Bev had told Mom once not to be surprised if she saw someone do that on their deathbed. Her friend Agnes had told her it's what the Italians call *la miglioria della morte*, which means "the improvement at the time of death." Mom called a priest from Pablo's parish, who had already anointed Pablo several days ago while he lay comatose, but Mom thought there might be a possibility of Confession and Communion, since Pablo had regained consciousness. Instead of the parish priest, a small, elderly, bent priest hobbled through the ICU door, his arm supported by a middle-aged Carmelite sister.

"I am honored to finally meet the family of my dear old friend," said Father Tomas in a crackly voice. "He has told me so much about all of you."

He reached out his hand to each of us and called us by name, guessing every one of us with uncanny accuracy. Mom, Dad, me, Laura, Katie and then John.

"Father, how long have you known Pablo?" I asked.

"Close to sixty years. We saved each other's lives. But that is a very long story. I will tell you after I administer the sacraments to my old friend."

He went to Pablo and picked up his hand. He bent in close to his ear and whispered in a gravelly voice. "Hello, my old friend. I have been blessed to know you. They say you will be leaving us soon to go to our Father's house. I will see you there, my friend. When I ring the doorbell, answer it."

A smile crept across Pablo's face. His eyes remained closed and did not open again until he received Communion, at which time he sat up in bed as if he had decided to get up and go for a walk.

He stretched out his hand straight in front of him and cast his eyes on whatever he was reaching for. "Lily," he gasped. "My beautiful Lily." Then, he lay down and closed his eyes, a soft peace settling on his face. The machine at his bedside let out one long, steady, definitive, unrelenting, nauseating beep.

Mom put her head on his hand and sobbed.

My phone vibrated. It was home. I went into the hallway to take the call. When I returned to the room, everyone was still in the exact same position. They all turned to look at me through their tears.

"Lily is gone," I said, folding my phone.

The weeping intensified.

"She went into cardiac arrest about a half hour ago. Danny called 911 but they couldn't bring her back."

"A half hour ago?" Katie said. "So, then, Pablo did see her."

"They're together now," Laura agreed.

Mom had been swept up into a cruel torrent of unbearable grief.

Hysteria had overtaken the sobbing as it does when someone loses a child.

"What am I going to do without my Lily?" She doubled to the floor. "What am I going to do? What am I going to do? What am I going to do?" She rocked as Dad cradled her trembling body. None of us predicted this intensity of grief. The loss of Pablo and Lily on the same day scared me as I watched my mother, wondering if she would ever recover. Wondering how she could.

"It's OK, Mom," I said, rubbing her back. "It's OK."

But I really didn't know how it ever could be.

Father prayed a Hail Mary for Pablo and one for Lily. Then he prayed, "May the souls of the faithful departed, through the mercy of God, rest in peace. Amen."

He ambled to Mom and raised his hand over her head. "God bless you, my little daughter. God grant you peace."

"Father," Laura said, bending to speak into his ear. "Would you pray for my daughter. She is ill."

"Of course," he said. "What is her name."

"Julie. She is seven."

"Julie," he smiled reassuringly. "What is wrong with her?"

"Her liver is failing."

"Julie will be in my prayers." He squeezed Laura's hand.

Sister whispered something in Father's ear.

"It's OK, Sister," he said.

"Now, Father, please."

"Do you need to tend to something else, Father?" Katie asked. "It's OK. We have each other."

"I'm afraid sister has appointed herself guardian of my health, and she is every bit as vigilant as the pain in my chest. She insists that I go take my medicine." He smiled and grabbed his chest, before raising his hand in blessing over us. "I will see you at the funeral."

"Will you be celebrating the Mass, Father?" Katie asked.

"Father James and I will concelebrate," he said. "I can no longer see to say Mass. But I will be there at the altar of our Lord."

"You are visually impaired?" asked Katie.

"Only about 90 percent blind."

"Then, how did you know us?" she asked.

"Like I said, Pablo told me about you. He loved you so very much." A layer of tears pooled around his whitened corneas. "So very much."

৪০୬cৠ୬৪୦୬cৠ୬৪୦୬cৠ୬৪୦୬cৠ

There was some discussion about flying Lily's body to Burbank so she could be buried with Jen Eagan and Pablo Perez.

But it was decided she belonged with Auntie Bev and her be-loved Frank back in Seattle. So Danny contacted Father Fitz and made arrangements for Lily's funeral to be held on Saturday.

First, we had to bury Pablo. Father Tomas gave the homily. This is the story the 99-year-old priest told of how he and Pablo met:

Pablo hadn't been to church since coming to America. One day while taking out the trash at a vocational skills school where he worked, he heard a woman screaming. He took off running in the direction of the cries for help. He was joined by several auto body students, who had also heard the screams. The men found a knife-wielding maniac outside the church gates. A priest and a middle-aged woman were collapsed, but still conscious, on the bloody asphalt. Two of the students stayed to help them, while Pablo and two others chased after the weaselly assailant. Pablo was able to catch up to him and pin him to the sidewalk in front of a favorite greasy spoon. The newspaper reporters and televi-sion crews clamored for interviews. Pablo and the students became short-term celebrities. Everyone loves a story about an everyday guy, rising to heroic heights.

The newspaper said that the woman, a church employee, had been opening the church gate when the assailant came up behind her and stabbed her for unknown reasons. The pastor came to her aid and the attacker turned his aggressions on him.

The injuries were not life threatening and the two victims recovered.

After the priest got out of the hospital, he made a trip to the vocational school to meet the men who had raced to the scene to help. He shook their hands, gave them each a blessed olive-wood cross from the Holy Land and promised to pray for them at Holy Mass. He looked Pablo in the eye when he said, "I will pray for your special intentions. Maybe I will see you at Mass sometime. Come this Sunday to the 10 a.m. and I will be able to take you out to lunch after."

Out of those five men, three showed up and took the priest up on his offer of lunch. Within two years, all three of them had become regular attendees at Mass.

After the story ran in the paper, the publisher offered Pablo a job as head janitor. And that is where he met a young woman and the two of them conceived Lily, whom Pablo loved so much that he fought off death long enough to enter into eternity with her, I'm sure hand-in-hand together.

The priest that Pablo saved was Father Tomas. And through Pablo's selfless and heroic act, he himself was also saved. Father Tomas had the honor of watching Pablo grow spiritually for many years.

"I lived long enough to witness, many decades after we met, how Pablo became devout in his Faith, embracing the teachings of the Church as they pertain to the way a man is meant to live his life," said Father Tomas. "And now, his loved ones can take comfort in that knowledge. Pablo loved the Lord. And his long journey to Him is now complete. May he rest in peace, basking in eternal Light."

After the funeral, Father Tomas came to me and laid his hand on my forearm.

"How are you holding up, my little daughter?"

"I am OK," I said. "I am very worried about my mother, though."

"She is a strong woman. Do not worry."

"You know, Father, Pablo never told us about saving you."

"That's Pablo."

"Makes me wonder how many other things we don't know about him."

"Undoubtedly many. But some day you will."

"Someday?"

"After this life."

"Oh," I said. "Yes."

"You don't believe that, do you?"

"Believe? You mean in Heaven?"

"Yes."

I felt him read my soul. I knew there was no use telling him what he wanted to hear.

"I don't know," I said. "I don't know if I will get there, even if there is one."

"You can get there, Beth. But only by Providence."

"Providence?"

"Like what happened to Pablo. In every life, there is some-one sent to reach across the chasm."

I thought of Father Fitz. And Danny.

"What if you don't reach back?"

"Sometimes you can't reach back. Sometimes you are too weak. A lost sheep, wounded and entangled in thorns, does not reach back. That's why a shepherd's staff is long with a crook at the end."

# 12

## Feeding the Unfeedable

I had been over to my parents' house several times since foster baby Carla had come to live with them. So I felt more than a little dread when my mother asked the favor.

"Listen, Beth Baby, I hate to ask you this, with all that you've got going on, but would you be able to watch Carla for a few hours Monday? I've got to go to take your father in for his colonoscopy."

"Well, I guess I could," I said. "But I'm a little afraid of all those tubes and wires. And she cries a lot. Not that I mind, I just wouldn't know what to do for her."

"It's not tubes and wires, Honey. It's just an apnea monitor. No big deal. I know she cries a lot. She just itches because of the liver disease. We won't be gone for that long, but I don't want to take her to sit in that doctor's office with all those germs when her immune system is so fragile. I can just drop her by on our way and pick her up on our way back."

"OK, sure, Mom. I don't mind. But is Laura not available?"

"No, she's volunteering at the school."

I didn't ask about Katie because none of us were going to dish out any more on Katie's plate. She had been working close to full time since Nick was killed three years ago. He pulled someone over in a routine traffic stop and the passenger shot him in the face.

Nick and Katie's two kids are finally now school age, so it has made it a little easier. Mom has been watching them just about every day while Katie tries to rebuild her life. She is doing quite a proficient job of rebuilding, I must say. And it seems she will soon have a two-parent household again. Apparently, someone had been watching her from afar as she took her two small children to Mass nearly every day. When her husband died, that someone took pity on her, I guess you could say, except that wouldn't be accurate. Katie is quite a catch and any man would be fortunate to have her. But I say, "take pity" because Gary is compassion incarnate. Nick was a good man. A very good man. Gary is a saint. Katie never knew Gary well until after Nick's death. He approached her at Mass one day, offered his condolences, pressed his phone number into her hand and told her if there's anything at all she needs – ever – no matter what time of day or night, she was to call him. Coincidentally, soon after that, someone anonymously set up a scholarship fund for the children, putting $5,000 in to get it going.

Katie has, and has always had, an uncommon strength, so she tucked the scrap of paper in her address book and never called the number. She didn't need someone to take care of her or her children. In addition to working at the medical lab on alternating weekends, Katie was fortunate enough to land a part-time job as the church secretary after Nick's death, which meant she could continue attending daily Mass, which meant she would continue to see Gary there every day, which meant Gary was a very happy fellow. You'd have to know Katie to understand. She is goodness – solid to her core. And out of all of us, she is the one who looks most like Mom. So I don't need to go into detail on her stunning physical attributes.

"Listen, Beth," Mom said. "I can reschedule Dad's appointment if you're uneasy about taking care of the baby. It's just a routine exam." Dad has colon cancer in his family, so he gets checked yearly.

"No, Mom, that's OK. I'll be fine with her."

"Oh, yeah," she said. "You can handle anything."

"No, Mom. You're getting me confused with Katie."

"Well, I don't raise any wimps."

Mom dropped off the baby with a bottle, several diapers, a change of clothes and three pacifiers, none of which worked to keep Carla happy. Unexplained liver failure in children has been on the increase in the past two or three decades. A new liver offered Carla's only hope of feeling well again, but she couldn't get on the organ transplant list until she reached 11 pounds. She had almost four pounds to go. She needed to bulk up before her liver gave out. Unlike kidneys, there is no substitute for the liver. Once your own fails, your only hope is to get someone else's. Sucking in calories was going to be Carla's route to survival. So I made certain to give her every last bit of the contents of her bottle, down to the last nipple full. I put her head against my shoulder to burp her and she turned her face into my neck, rolling her yellowed eyes all the way to their corners to find my eyes. Her fragile helplessness grabbed at my insides. If she hadn't been so yellow, so noisy and so miserable, she would have been gorgeous. Even through her contorted face, I could see the beauty in her dainty features – a tiny, slightly turned up nose, heart-shaped lips and very long eyelashes. When Mom came to pick Carla up, she grabbed the empty bottle off the counter and looked at me in a state of shock.

"What's wrong," I asked.

"Did she drink all of this?"

"Yes," I said. "That's the bottle you told me to give her."

"Yes, I know," she said. "But it's usually a struggle to get even half of it down her."

"I did notice she is a sluggish eater," I said. "But she kept going."

"How did you do it?" she asked.

"I don't know," I said. "Nothing special. I just put the nipple in her mouth and she sucked."

"Well, how were you holding her? Show me."

I picked the baby up and demonstrated my "technique." "I think, like this."

"That's amazing," she said. "You know she has an appointment next week to have a feeding tube put in because she's not gaining weight fast enough. She just doesn't want to eat."

"Well, she wanted to today," I said.

"It's almost time for her next feeding. Would you try to feed her again? I want to see what she does."

"Yeah, sure," I shrugged.

Carla ate the whole bottle in what Mom said was about half the time of her usual feeding.

"Maybe she's turned a corner," I said.

"Maybe," Mom smiled. "Oh, it would be so wonderful. Those feeding tubes can make it so hard on the apnea. Remember Cecelia had to be resuscitated when they first put her on one? I just would hate for Carla to have to have one if we can fatten her up the old fashioned way."

Mom tried for two days after that to duplicate the angle at which I had held her head and the incline at which I had positioned her body. Carla ate less than half her bottle at each feeding. Mom asked me to come over and feed her. Carla sucked it all down.

"Honey, I know this is a lot to ask. But could you take Carla for a little while. Obviously, she will only eat for you. And she really needs to eat."

"What about the shelter?"

"I'll fill in for you."

So I temporarily traded lives with my mother. Carla gained an ounce a day, reaching eleven pounds seven weeks later. She underwent a liver transplant, which her body accepted well. She thrived.

Ever since then, I've been legendary in the Lovely family as the one who saved Carla's life.

"Beth was the only one that baby would eat for," Mom would tell everyone. "They had some kind of special connection. We still can't explain it, but God knew what he was doing when he brought those two souls together, that's for sure."

This was the story she told while standing with a group of friends at Lily's wake. It was an appropriate story for Lily's wake because, if it wasn't for Lily, Carla would have never been in our lives. Mom and Dad became foster parents because they wanted Lily to have little ones to love since she wouldn't be able to have any of her own.

The story of Carla stirred an uneasiness inside me every time Mom told it. Mom believes that every person is put on the earth to do some kind of good and that Carla is just one example of the good I have done. But at the core of the Carla story, as archived in my mind, was its antithesis – namely that, while I had done good to one life, I had destroyed another. And so I cringed internally at the telling and retelling of my heroic deed, which really consisted of little more than putting a nipple in a baby's mouth. I really didn't even have an authentic attachment to Carla. No emotional one anyway. I wanted her to survive. I wanted it very badly. But mostly because I knew she deserved to. Not because I felt anything more for her than I do any other baby wheeled by me in a stroller at the mall.

Mom's ordeal with Carla has, I think, made it particularly hard for her to handle Julie's condition. Having been privy to all the medical details of failing livers, Mom just simply knows too much. She knows the Carla story could have had a very different outcome.

The wake ended gradually as friends kissed us and trickled out.

While Danny helped Dad wrap things up with the funeral home staff, I asked Mom to take a walk with me. I knew she still needed to talk about her sister. Talking about her would be akin to being with her.

"Mom, what was it like growing up with Aunt Lily?"

"It was never dull."

"Was she mischievous?"

"No, not mischievous. But she did get into mischief. Your grandma used to say that Lily didn't go looking for trouble be-cause she and trouble shared the same address. An address which, by the way, should never have been stocked with permanent markers."

Mom laughed and shook her head as she watched her feet move along the sidewalk.

"I remember we worked so hard to get Lily to write her name," she said. "It was always a little off. Lil or Lli or Lly or Lyli or iLly. One day, it finally clicked and Lily wrote in beautiful, perfectly formed large print – *Lily*. The accomplishment was met with some mixed emotion from Auntie Bev, however. Lily's spelling epiphany had been demonstrated in black Sharpie, right over the couch on the family room wall. I held my breath and waited. Frustration flashed in Auntie Bev's eyes. And then this wide smile broke out on her face and she said, 'By golly, she spelled it right!' She clapped her hands together once and held that pose in front of her chest, as if she was in prayer, in grateful thanksgiving or something. And then there was, from that day forward, a permanent ban on permanent markers."

Mom and I both chuckled. And then walked for a moment in silence.

"Mom, I just want to let you know. I know I've caused you many sleepless nights. And I know I haven't always been your pride and joy. But I want you to know, I will always be there for you. I will take care of you. When you're old and forgetful or you need your diaper changed, I'll be there."

Mom hugged me hard and buried her face in my shoulder. When she came up, I noticed she had tears in her eyes. "I know you will, Honey. I know you will. It's the kind of person you are."

That's when I realized just how weak Mom was at that moment. Though I meant every word I said, I fully expected a smart aleck response to the diaper offer. I had never seen my mother vulnerable before. She is like one of those mighty redwoods. There might be something that can knock her to the ground, but it wouldn't be anything within the realm of the ordinary.

"Auntie Bev was fortunate enough to have Lily with her in her last hours. I was hoping for the same thing. I know I shouldn't have assumed I'd go before Lily, since we're so close in age, but I just never contemplated a life without her. She has always been my little sister. It's not right that she is gone."

"You were expecting her to recover, weren't you?"

"I learned a long time ago not to make expectations on anyone's lifespan," she said. "But, I was praying."

"God had a plan. "

She looked at me, sort of stunned. I think she was surprised to hear me mention God. She can thank Danny for that. Although I wouldn't say he has brought me back to the Faith, he has brought a bit of faith back to me.

Danny had invited me to church quite a number of times, but I always had something else going. He tried to entice me to go to Confession, but I knew I could never tell anyone what I had done. I could not say the words. Not even in my room alone with the door closed. My mouth refused and I was glad because even *I* did not want to hear them.

"How are things between you and Danny?" Mom asked, strangely enough, while I was thinking about him.

"Tentative," I said.

"Well, that's the way it is sometimes," she said. "When your Dad and I were dating, I was never quite sure he was going to call for another date. One night, in his car, as I collected my purse from the floor by my feet, I noticed my purse had tipped, and my check book had fallen out and was sticking out from under the seat. I instinctively reached my hand down to grab it and then stopped. Leave it, I told myself, and you will be certain to see him again."

"Nice trick," I said.

"In my experience, all relationships need some kind of insurance policy," she winked. "If you don't have a marriage license, a lost checkbook will have to do."

# 13

## Holy Coyote

Mom asked me to deliver the eulogy. I didn't want to, but I knew I should. I knew there would be no one better. Not because I am a good story teller. But because of the story I had to tell, which was this:

I grew up 1,399 miles away in Minneapolis, with a vague idea of who my Aunt Lily was. I knew she was different. I knew she was slow. I knew she was nice because the two times I remember meeting her, she had a big smile for me. When I was 14 years old, my parents told me we were moving to Seattle to take care of Aunt Lily. I was not happy about this. In fact, I was distraught. My parents thought I was upset because I didn't want to leave my boyfriend. The truth is, that boyfriend had, several weeks before, lost interest in courting me. And now I was courting death. My best friend, Caroline, and I were making a plan. This will come as a shock to my family, because I have never told them. This friend and I were planning to drive out into the woods, park by a lake and take too many pills. We were going to do this on July 12 – the anniversary of the day we had met. We had planned not to leave any notes. We wanted it to look like an accidental overdose so our families would suffer no guilt or any additional pain beyond that caused by the death of a child. I really didn't want to cause anyone any pain, but I couldn't figure out how else to alleviate mine. So these were the plans we talked about every day after school as we got high, smoking grass and popping pills. When Mom told me we were moving, I figured Caroline and I would have a bit of time to revise our plans. But the house sold quickly, and before I knew it, we were all packed into an SUV heading for Seattle. Caroline never went through with our plan either and grew up to be a drug counselor. I'm sure Caroline's life has changed many others. Maybe my life will too. Or maybe even one. That would be enough.

ℰℭℰℭℰℭℰℭℰℭℰℭℰℭ

Dad cried for the first time at the grave site. I wrapped my arms around his middle and cried with him. I felt his large frame tremble against me as he tried to hold back the majority of his grief. Of course, it was raining. Danny stood at my other side, his hands in his overcoat pockets, his head bowed slightly. Katie and Laura stood on either side of Mom.

As the crowd dispersed, John stayed, looking on at the casket. Danny and I watched him from a distance for a few minutes. John is a large man like Dad, but he looked peculiarly slight at that moment among the thriving madrona trees, well watered through the years by the tears of unbearable losses.

"I'll be right back," I told Danny. "Why don't you go on to the car. I'll meet you."

My three-inch heels poked hole after hole into the soft soil. I laid my hand on John's shoulder. He remained still like a statue, apparently finding it unnecessary to turn and see who had touched him.

"You don't want to say good-bye, do you?" I said.

"I don't know how," he said, without expression.

"Then don't. She's still with you."

"She used to shove cake and cookies in her purse and bring them to me when Mom sent me to my room. Never used Saran Wrap. Just shoved them in there."

"She had a big heart," I said. "Especially for you."

I held onto him as the tears came pouring out. As rare as thunder is in Seattle, we ignored the clapping sky, but started walking, arm in arm, when we heard the limo's ignition.

The reception was at my parents' house, catered by a friend of Danny's who owns an Italian deli. When we got to the house, the two bathrooms on the main floor were immediately occupied. I went to the one in the basement. Every time I am in that bathroom, I think of the friendship between Lily and Timbledee Sniff. Mom spent a good part of her life trying to get that hamster out of something. There was the time he crawled inside a hole in John's car seat and didn't have enough room to turn around and come back out. It was on that day that we learned -- as we watched Mom try for more than an hour to pry moulded plastic open at the seams with a flat-head screwdriver -- that car seats are, as they should be, virtually indestructible. Except when there's a small creature with near-celebrity status trapped inside.

But the most costly and harrowing rescue of Timbledee Sniff was necessary only because of one single and uncharacteristic instance of home maintenance neglect that occurred shortly after the hamster came to live with us. An interior designer by trade, Mom has a keen eye for detail, so how it went unnoticed that John's room was missing a doorstop is still a mystery to this day. But, because there was no door stop, there was, of course, a doorknob sized hole behind John's door. And because there was a hole, there was, of course, the temptation to deposit a hamster into it. And because there was a temptation, there was, of course, a little boy who could not resist it. So, we in the Lovely household were immediately faced with a difficult question. How, exactly, does one go about getting a hamster out of a wall? Which led to the more practical questions: *Does* one go about getting a hamster out of a wall? Or does one simply spend $7 on a new hamster? How late is the pet store open? What are the ethical implications of the answers to all these questions? And finally, will there be a stench?

But when you have Lily talking to the hamster through the wall, telling him he's going to be OK, reassuring him that help is on the way and that all of us love him very much, there is really only one answer, (which sounds a bit Reaganesque, now that I think about it). *Tear down that wall.*

So Mom got out her hack saw. Meanwhile, Lily grew increasingly concerned that Timbledee would clumsily stumble into the path of the long, sharp blade slicing through the drywall and she would never hold her little friend again. This would have been tragic because Lily and Timbledee shared quite a bond. We actually got him for John as a reward for pooping in the potty, but Lily named him, based on her inability to remember and pronounce "Timothy." Timby, as he was called most of the time, got along with John, but he loved Lily. We knew this because he allowed only Lily to lay him on his back in her hand. He even occasionally groomed while lying there, wiping his face with his hand-like paws.

Lily had refused to touch Timbledee when we first brought him home. But she soon realized that the new pet had the most endearing combination of features a small, holdable creature can have – soft, silky fur, like a bunny; a disproportionately large, very pink nose; ears with visible veins; a body that alternately stretched and scrunched depending on the task at hand; and skin that was at least three sizes too big. All that skin, by the way, remained unscathed, thanks to Mom's precision with a saw and her ability to hear exactly where Timbledee was scratching the insulation.

The next time that hamster set out on an adventure, he made it much easier on us – as easy, in fact, as making a sandwich. After a day and a half at large, Timbledee was found lodged inside a loaf of French bread. He had nibbled his way into the middle and was quite content there, apparently unaware that bread, at some point, gets sliced. At least it does in America. Fortunately, Mom noticed a strange heaviness to that particular loaf and investigated before taking a knife to it.

The reason I was thinking about all of this in the basement bathroom, while the bereaved ate cold cuts and consoled each other above my head, is because of several pry marks in the little strip of wood that joins the cabinet to the wall. One day, Timbledee Sniff found a hole where the vertical and horizontal pieces of wood did not quite meet in the built-in cabinet. Mom had to pry a piece of wood off to rescue the rodent, who was not at all in favor of being rescued from the narrow, tunnel-like space he had found between the cabinet and the wall. Timbledee planted himself just out of reach of Mom's hand, chewing on a piece of scrap wood some careless carpenter had left behind in the building of the home. Mom called Timbledee. John called him. Laura and Katie and I called him. We tried to bait him out with a carrot and then a Cheerio and then a sunflower seed. These were on his list of favorites. He ignored us and chewed. No surprise. We all speculated that when a hamster is chewing he has no better chance of hearing you or smelling food than a man does when he is watching football. It wasn't until he heard Lily's voice calling "Timby, come here, Timby," that he dropped his new-found chew stick and froze. Within seconds he had ambled his way into her hands.

When I came back upstairs from the bathroom, I made myself a sandwich, even though I wasn't hungry. Mom got up out of her chair, where she had been sitting with Jimmy and Dad, came to me and hugged me tight. She suggested we go sit on the back porch. She wanted to know why I never told her about my plans to end my life.

"That was a long time ago, Mom," I said, biting into a pepperoncini.

"You never feel like that anymore?"

"No," I said. "Never."

"Are you sure, Honey? You need to tell me if you ever do. I'll help you. Through anything, Honey. Through anything. You know that."

"I know, Mom."

"Why did you want to take your own life, Honey?"

"I don't know," I said, putting the pepperoncini tail on my plate. "It wasn't rational."

"It scares me."

"Don't be scared," I said. "It was a long time ago."

"It scares me to think what would have happened if we hadn't moved. You know who you have to thank for that, don't you? Your father. He's the one who talked me into moving so we could take care of Lily."

"I love that man," I said.

"Me too." Mom took an obligatory bite of her sandwich. "Beth, did you ever feel like I didn't love you?"

"No," I said. "You have always been a great Mom."

"There was a period of time when I was just so numb, so void of emotions. I just hope you and your sisters never interpreted that as a lack of love."

"No," I said. "We always knew you were in our corner. I don't think I ever knew, though, that you would love me no matter what. Now I know. But I don't think kids know that."

"If kids don't know that, all sorts of horrible things can happen," Mom said. "You know, I once heard a wise woman at a foster care conference say that every child needs one person who is crazy about them. Just one person. But that person has to love them to the point of insanity."

"I'd say you're pretty insane when it comes to kids, Mom, whether they be yours or someone else's."

"Remember Charlie?"

"Oh, yes," I said. "No one could forget Charlie. She was quite a piece of work."

"Made in the image of God, but disfigured by a cruel humanity."

"But you restored her, Mom. How did you do that?"

"Crazy love."

The first time Mom told Charlie she loved her, Charlie was offended.

"What does that mean?" she said with an elevated nose and lowered eyelids.

"What does what mean?" Mom asked. "What does love mean?"

"You don't even know me. How can you say that you love me?" It was a confrontation more than an actual quest for understanding.

"No one's ever said that to you before, have they?"

"I'll answer your question if you'll answer mine."

"What question? What is love?"

"No, I know what love is. Why would you say you love me?"

"Because I do. What do you think it means?"

"Love?"

"Yes."

"I could tell you my answer, but I'm sure you'd tell me I'm wrong. Why don't you enlighten me."

"Well, it doesn't mean liking everything someone does or being impressed with everything they say. That would be called admiration. Love is a completely different thing altogether."

"So, you've educated me on what love is not. I already know what love is not. I've seen too stinking much of what love is not."

"OK. So now I'll tell you what love is." Mom waited for Charlie to look into her face.

"It means wanting all the best things for someone."

Charlie just stared.

"And," Mom said.

"And?"

"And giving everything you can to help them get it."

"Like a new Ferrari?"

"No. That's not one of the best things."

"So, what are the best things?"

"Faith, hope and love."

Charlie looked puzzled and annoyed.

"You've never had these things, have you?"

She shrugged and turned her head toward the window.

"Come on, Charlie. You said if I answer your question, you'll answer mine."

"No."

"You're not going to answer?"

"No, I've never had those things."

"Is it wrong for me to want you to have them?"

"No. It's not wrong."

"Then, your original question has been answered. That's why I said I love you."

The psychologists say that once a baby reaches the age of six months without having bonded with another human being, he will never bond with anyone his entire life. Mom says that theory would hold up were it not for the merciful healing of God and the real possibility of miracles. Mom never discounts these possibilities. I've never known her to consider any soul lost.

"How did you know what answers to give that girl?" I asked.

"You prepared me well, Beth. Her questions were easy. Yours weren't. And I get the feeling you still haven't found all the answers. Have you, Beth?"

"Not quite all of them, Mom, no."

"Maybe I can help you find the answers."

"I don't think anyone can, Mom."

"One thing I've learned in all my years, there's no such thing as a difficult answer. We make all the important questions difficult. But the answers are always quite simple."

"Really?"

"Sure, try me. Ask me anything."

"Why does the sun rise?"

"Love."

"Love?"

"God keeps the Earth rotating on its axis out of love for His creatures."

"Why do people suffer?"

"Love."

"Love."

"Suffering is a route to holiness, which allows us to make it to Heaven and have eternal happiness. Who other than someone who loves us would want us to have that?"

"Why do people kill?"

"Love."

"Oh, come on now."

"God gave us free will because he loves us and wants us to freely choose to love Him."

"Love is your answer to every question."

"Now you've got it. See how simple it is?"

I rolled my eyes. "Let's go in and look at the pictures of Lily," I said, folding my plate with my half eaten sandwich.

For the funeral reception, Mom had set up a table in the living room with a number of beautiful photos: a school picture of Lily as a girl about 8, wearing ponytails tied in red bows on each side of her head, missing two front teeth. A snapshot of her as a baby with a puppy licking her chin. A picture of her grown up, hugging Pablo. Both are beaming at the camera, wearing balloon sculpture hats. A picture of Lily stooping over Auntie Bev's wheelchair, arms wrapped around her neck. A wedding portrait of Lily and Frank.

You would have assumed that Lily and Frank would have met at a group home or a day program or in the Special Olympics. But that would have been the normal way two people like Lily and Frank meet. That would not have been the fairy tale way. And God must have noticed that Lily deserved a fairy tale.

So there Lily was, traveling alone on a 737 bound to Burbank to visit Pablo. We had tried to get her a window seat because she loved to watch the houses and trees growing ever smaller until the plane climbed through the clouds to cruising altitude. Then she liked to pretend that the clouds below are places for the angels to rest, like celestial beanbag chairs. But there was no window seat available, so Lily had to settle for an aisle, 29C. It would be nearly impossible to believe who was seated directly across the aisle, unless you believe in the theory that some things are just meant to be. There in 29D sat Frank

Stillwell from Vancouver, B.C., bound for Burbank to visit relatives and ride California Screamin', determined to make good on a $5 bet he made with his best friend, who predicted Frank would be too scared to get on it, considering it had broken down the last time he rode it and all the passengers had to be rescued from his train 120 feet in the air.

After their plane reached cruising altitude, Frank told Lily that California Screamin' opened on the day he was born. He also told her that the coaster is 6,072 feet long, travels 55 mph, lasts 2.36 minutes, accelerates from 0-55 in four seconds and carries 24 passengers per train. A loaded train weighs 22,000 pounds. The trains depart every 36 seconds and travel 55,000 miles per year. You must be at least 48 inches to ride, which meant Frank had to wait until he was 12. The coaster requires six miles of electrical wire. The manufacturer is Intamin AG.

Lily listened to all of this with great interest, even though she's not allowed to ride roller coasters anymore because of her heart condition.

"I have a heart condition too," Frank said.

"What kind do you have?" Lily asked.

"VSD," said Frank, beaming with pride. "But I still ride roller coasters."

"Me too," Lily exclaimed. "I have that kind too!"

And from that moment on, they knew their hearts were meant for one another.

By the time the plane had touched down, Frank had proposed to Lily. She said she had to ask her father, which worked out great, because she happened to be on her way to see him. She took Frank's phone number and promised to call. Frank said he would like to come see her in Burbank and that maybe he should be the one to ask her father for permission to marry her. He had seen that done in an old movie once and the father had said yes, so it must be the way to go. Or, Lily suggested, Frank could just ask her father at the airport because her father will be picking her up.

The two were beaming when they disembarked, hand-in-hand, Lily stretching her neck to see over people's heads, looking for Pablo, with great hope in her heart, starting her vacation and starting the rest of her life.

Lily was married at St. James Cathedral because she had seen the cathedral on television one Palm Sunday when she was too sick to go to Mass. She said it was the most beautiful place she had ever seen and she resolved, as she watched the televised Mass, that she would be married there someday. None of us ever thought we would see the day. Indeed, the church, lined down the center aisle with white lilies, was breathtaking – even more so in real life than on television. Frank moved in with Lily, in a guest house Mom and Dad had built for them. The couple lived there in a smartly decorated one-bedroom cottage in the back yard, behind Mom and Dad and John and the three to five foster children that lived there at any given moment.

While the rest of us knew their marriage would be childless and tried to give Lily a crash course in rudimentary statistics and probabilities, Lily kept waiting for a baby. The doctors had recommended sterilization, but we knew the highly slim odds of conception for two people with their particular disabilities. Besides, sterilization is a topic that gets no airtime in our home, given Mom and Dad's past. They had lived it and grown to loathe it. So the possibility of Lily bearing a child always remained open, albeit infinitesimal.

About two years after Lily and Frank were married, it was discovered that Frank had Alzheimer's. He deteriorated quickly and the disease ended up taking his life two years after that. Lily had experienced her share of loss in her life, but I don't think she ever truly recovered from that one. She once said that if it wasn't for John, she would wish to die immediately so she could go to Heaven and see Frank. But she knew John needed her, so she had to stay.

It was a decade after Frank's death, when she moved in with me. During the process of unpacking, I found Lily sitting in her closet, rocking and crying into a red and blue striped rugby shirt she had clutched to her chest.

"Lily, what's wrong," I asked.

"I can- smell Frank anymore," she said. "See?" She held the shirt to my nose. "A long time ago, it smell like Frank."

This was the shirt Frank was wearing on the airplane when he and Lily first met. It is the one piece of his clothing she chose not to donate to the Special Olympics thrift store. It is the shirt that was Lily's dance partner nearly every evening after Frank died. She would put on the Turtles' *So Happy Together*, loud enough to disturb the sockeye salmon in Puget Sound and she and that old shirt would twirl round and round together, the shirt frolicking much taller than she at some moments and caught in her embrace at others. Sometimes Lily would join in the chorus. *I can't see me lovin' nobody but you for all my life.* It was the tune Lily and Frank danced to at their wedding reception, after the D.J. announced, "Ladies and Gentlemen, Mr. and Mrs. Stillwell," and the guests applauded and kept applauding until Lily could get her bracelet untangled from the snag in Mom's purple lace matron of honor dress, remove her white high-heeled pumps and waddle onto the dance floor, arm-in-arm with her first and only beloved.

Lily was right about the shirt. It smelled like generic fabric, not like someone.

"I'm sorry, Lily," I said. "I washed all your clothes as we were unpacking them. I didn't realize it would ruin the smell of Frank's shirt. Can you forgive me?"

"Yes, I forgive you," she sniffed, wiping both eyes at once with her thumb and forefinger.

That's when I realized I couldn't mess with any of Lily's stuff. She needed her own space, just like all the rest of us. She had special things and they smelled a certain way and she wanted that to remain a constant.

"I'm sorry, Lily," I said, putting my arm around her. "I know you miss him."

I knew how Lily loved Frank because I had loved someone like that once. Like nothing beautiful ever ends: that's how the young love.

ಐ๒ৎ✿ಐ๒ৎ✿ৎ✿ಐ๒৮✿ৎ✿ಐ๒ৎ✿ৎ

After almost everyone had gone home from the funeral reception, Laura and Katie sat on either side of Mom, looking through photos of when we were kids. Paul and Gary had taken the kids home.

Dad was scouring the house for paper plates and plastic tumblers and stuffing them into a large garbage bag. He looked as tired as I'd ever seen him. I joined his efforts and he squeezed my shoulder as I tossed trash into the bag.

"Hey, Beth, what do say we grab a beer and go for a walk?" he said.

The sky had cleared and there was a salmon pinkness to the horizon. It provided a nice distant focal point for two exhausted people to trudge toward in blinkless stares.

"How are you holding up, Beth?"

"I'm OK," I said.

We scuffed along for a while in silence. I know I speak for both of us when I say our feet felt like wet sponges sludging through molasses.

"You probably don't remember me saying I love you very often, do you Beth?"

"Actually, never," I said.

Dad looked at me with an expression somewhere between puzzled and shocked.

"Well, I'm sorry about that, Beth," he said. "Because I really do."

"I know," I said, taking his arm and squeezing his bicep.

"You're just not the mushy type. You inherited that from me."

"You have no idea how much, though, Beth."

"How much what?" I said.

"You know. How much I– How much I want to wring your neck right now."

"What for?"

"For trying to me make me say it."

"Say what?"

"Elizabeth Rose Lovely."

"Yes?"

"You really want to hear it, don't you?"

"I really do," I said. "But I'll settle for vague phrases like 'you have no idea how much I do.'"

"Did you ever doubt my love for you?"

"There were long periods of time when I never thought about your love for me."

"Well, I thought about it constantly," he said. "You know. Especially when you were into all that trouble. I knew we could lose you, Beth. I knew that. It might have seemed like to you that I was oblivious, but I wasn't."

"No?"

"Do you know why we moved out here?"

"To take care of Lily."

"Yes, and for you."

"To get me away from that crowd I was hanging with."

"Yeah. And to get me away from someone too."

"Who?"

"What I'm about to tell you, Beth, I have not told anyone. Not even your mother. I probably shouldn't be telling you, but I want you to know how important you are to me. How important you've always been."

"OK, Dad," I said. "I can keep a secret. What were you, running from the Mafia or something?"

"There was this friend of mine back in Minneapolis. She worked with me on some projects for awhile. We became close, you know, emotionally. She wanted to have an affair, but I didn't want to. I stood my ground, but I didn't trust myself. I was always afraid I would fall, so I was more than happy when an opportunity came up to leave Minneapolis."

"Did you love her?"

"I'm sorry to say that I did. But she was not the kind of person your mother is. Not by a long shot. There is no comparing the level of character your mother has to any other woman. I didn't always see it that way. But after nearly forty years of marriage, I can tell you, without hesitation, your mother is in a league of her own. And I'm not even talking physical beauty here. But add that on too. There is no woman on the face of this earth who is more stunning in beauty than your mother."

"I know. So what more could you have wanted?"

"What happened – or almost happened – between me and that other woman is very typical, Beth. Things had gotten pretty stale between your mother and me. People let that happen to their marriages. I don't know why. They lose interest in each other. As if there's nothing new to learn about the other person any more. My friend made me feel interesting again. She wanted to know everything about me. That was exciting and very difficult to resist."

"But you did resist?"

"There was one thing that kept me faithful, Beth. I knew your mother would never tolerate infidelity, and I knew a broken home might put you over the edge. I feared that if your mother and I didn't stay together, you would fall apart. Katie would have survived it. Laura would have survived it. Your mother would have even survived it. You, I don't know. Every time I would be tempted, I'd think of you."

"Not of Mom?"

"You were the fragile one, Beth."

"I think you were correct," I said. "I don't know if I would have survived that."

"I know. That's why I'm so happy Lily brought us out here. If we hadn't moved, I don't know how much longer I could have resisted. You've got to understand, Beth. I did not want to have these feelings about another woman. But I did have them."

"Do you still think about her?"

"Yeah, but not in the way you might think. When I think about her it's because I'm trying to figure out what exactly I was drawn to. And the only thing I can come up with is that I was drawn to the person I thought I was when I was with her. I liked being the interesting guy that she thought I was."

I watched my feet pass over the ground.

"Do you wish I hadn't told you?" Dad asked, finally.

"Do you feel better for having told someone?"

"Only if it doesn't end up hurting you."

"No, it won't," I said. "And no, I don't wish you hadn't told me. You needed to tell somebody."

附♰附♰附♰附♰附♰附

Mom tried to get me to spend the night so I wouldn't have to be alone, but I really wanted my own bed. I intended to crash right into it after Danny dropped me off, but I had to walk past the box that Pablo had given me in order to get there. This was the first free moment I'd had since Pablo and Lily died and I was too curious to let the contents of the box wait until morning. Plus, I missed Pablo and wanted to be close to something he had owned. I put the box on my bed and ripped off the masking tape. Inside was an old quilt – a Mexican star quilt done in eggshell white, green and orange. It had been draped over the back of his couch when I had taken him home to Burbank and I had commented about how pretty it was. He told me a friend of his made it for him. There was also something wrapped in newspaper: a bull terrier inside a snow globe. Finally, there was a shoe box with an envelope inside. I opened it to find a cashier's check for $1,900. The note said it was all that he had and that I should spend it on whatever Lily and I might want.

Inside a shoe box marked, *For Lily, my precious daughter* was an envelope containing an unframed 4 by 6 of a litter of bull terrier puppies, mauling Pablo's face with a frolicking deluge of pink licks. Pablo's face was broad with laughter. I could hear it in my head. I remember how much comfort it would bring me.

To hear it was to know that all was right with the world. How I could use that right now.

"May the souls of the faithful departed, through the mercy of God, rest in peace," I whispered. I had committed that to memory when Pablo told it to me. I repeated it over and over again in my head as I fell asleep that night. Tonight it brought me comfort to be able to fulfill the request he had made of me.

I made the sign of the cross and kissed my hand like I had seen Pablo do so many times. He told me once that the cross was in honor of the Trinity and the kiss was for the Blessed Virgin.

In the bottom of the shoe box was another envelope that said, *To Lily: I give you my greatest treasure.* Inside was a small, round gold object that looked like an ancient piece of jewelry. It was shaped somewhat like a pedaled flower. It had a red center, covered in glass. Under the glass was a dark brown particle placed on top of a larger white dot. Next to the dot was a very small label, which read, *S. Toribio Romo.*

The next day, I brought it to Mom and asked her what it was. She said it is a relic, a tiny bone fragment of a saint. She had never heard of Saint Toribio Romo, so we looked him up online and learned that he is a Catholic priest who was killed by Mexican authorities during the Cristero War, which took place in the 1920s, when the Mexican government tried to cleanse the culture of all things Catholic. They confiscated Church property, executed many priests, exiled more and forbade all to say Mass or pray the Rosary in public. In the early morning of February 25, 1928, the government tracked down Father Romo in a factory where he had been hiding out with his sister, a nun. He was shot in his bed as he lay sleeping. He arose and took several steps. He was shot again and fell into the arms of his sister. She cried out, "Courage, Father Toribio ... merciful Christ, receive him! *Viva Cristo Rey,"* which means, "long live Christ the King."

Mom and I found a *Dallas Morning News* article about illegal immigrants who tell a common story. While making the treacherous journey across the desert, there appears a stranger –

a young  priest with piercing blue eyes, who gives them directions, water or money or tells them where to find work once they make it over the border. Sometimes he will even lead the way to safety.

One such immigrant asked the kindly priest where he might go to repay him once he found employment. The priest told him to ask for his whereabouts in Jalostitlan, Jalisco. After working for a while in California, the illegal did eventually return to Mexico to seek out the kind stranger. In Jalostitlan, he was told to go to the village of Santa Ana. The locals directed him to the church, upon which he discovered the picture of the man who had helped him hanging above the altar. It was Father Toribio Romo, who had been killed some fifty years earlier. Because of hundreds of stories like these, Father Romo has become known as the Patron Saint of Immigrants. He is, I supposed, in a manner of speaking, a holy coyote.

"Where in the world did Pablo get this?" I asked Mom.

"Typically, relics are given to you. You can't just order them on Amazon, that's for sure."

"I'll bet Father Tomas gave it to him," I said.

"I'll bet so," she said. "Well, now my dear, you have something very few people have. You have an honest- to-goodness, certified relic of the Catholic Church."

"Here, Mom. You should keep it."

"No, Honey. It's going to go to one of you kids anyway eventually and you were closest to Pablo. It's yours."

"What do I do with it?"

"Put it in a safe place. Cherish it. There just may come a day when you need a miracle."

# 14

# *Call it Even*

Since Lily's death, Buck wanted only to live in a corner. He hadn't eaten a thing. I decided it was time to bring Pablo's dogs home. I had them cared for at the shelter until I could get my bearings. Within twenty minutes of Badger and Ben Hur coming into the house, Buck was crunching kibbles. They all stood around the same bowl, wagging their tails and sharing a meal. There was not the usual play for dominance. They were as polite and distinguished as gentlemen at a black-tie affair, except they chewed with their mouths open.

Watching them made me miss mealtime companionship. Lily and I always ate breakfast and dinner together. Some people might have found her table manners unsavory. Her mouth was always overstuffed. Her lips and chin and fingers were covered in edible debris. But for me, her passion for food made everything taste so much better. To see someone enjoy food that much was to come to appreciate it in a way that most people never do. It was similar to listening to someone having a love affair with music play the piano. Or hearing a collector describe a beloved work of art. Or listening to a child retell a favorite movie. The admiration of another seems to raise the value of a commodity. That's what makes the free market system work, I guess. Since

Lily died, food just hadn't tasted so good. I needed what Buck now had: someone to eat with.

Although my friend Rebecca could not be that person, I decided to look her up for the purposes of nostalgia. She is the person I shared the most meals with for four years of my life. I found her e-mail address and sent her a brief note, asking if she remembers Professor Snell, who wore the same thing every day, leading his students to speculate about whether his clothing was actually a body tattoo. Though why anyone would want a tattoo of polyester brown pants and an earth-tone plaid shirt with faux pearl snaps was never discussed. Rebecca is the only best friend I've ever had in my adult life. We met in molecular biology class and would forge long hours into the night drilling each other on how to detect and quantify dehalococcoides and other bacteria.

In her senior year, she met a med student, and I was the maid of honor at their wedding. We had kept in contact up until she had her first child. That was seven years ago. I sent a Babies R Us gift card and talked about coming to see the baby. But I never did. We talked on the phone several more times throughout the first year of the baby's life and then we just stopped calling. Actually, I think Rebecca was the last one to put a call into me. I had called and left messages several times before that and so had she. I knew, as strong as our friendship once was, though, the minute I speak to her, it would not matter who was supposed to call back whom. It would be as if years had not passed. I planned to find out what her daughter was interested in and mail her a toy.

I told Danny this on a day hike at Mt. Rainier, and he shook his head in silence as he watched his hiking boots trudge up the rocky trail.

"What?" I asked.

"Oh, Beth, don't you see what you've done all your life?" He perched his walking stick into the ground and turned to look into my face. "Why'd you lose contact with Rebecca?"

"You know how life happens," I said, casually passing by him. "It just moves. It's hard to keep up with everything. We both got busy."

"You were avoiding her baby," he said, following close behind me.

"No," I said, still looking straight ahead. "She was my friend. I wouldn't have done that."

"Come on, Beth, it's me you're talking to. You don't have to pretend. I already know you're not OK."

"Not OK? Says you." I grunted the words as I heaved myself higher up the trail, pressing hard on my walking stick.

"I am not the only one who has noticed, Beth."

"Oh?"

"Do you know why Katie has gone to church every day for the last seven years?"

"No."

"You probably just chalked it up to religious fanaticism."

I shrugged.

"A crutch maybe?" Danny said.

"Boredom with life. Nothing else to do with all the kids. It was a way to get out of the house every day. Someplace to go. Be part of the community. Be with adults on a regular basis. She never went before the kids were born."

"No. It wasn't just an excuse to get out of the house."

We were walking side by side now. The trail had leveled out.

"So, what is the reason, oh great one, who knows all?"

"You."

"Me?"

"And how do you know that?"

"She told me. After Lily's funeral. She said she always knew you were suffering and never knew what to do about it."

"She never told me that. I've never said anything to her about my suffering."

"Beth, it's pretty obvious. You think you're living a normal life, but you're not. It's not normal to be in the kind of pain you are. So, after her babies were born and you wouldn't come to the hospital and hold them, it dawned on her that something was wrong. You know, Katie is very intuitive. She knows more things than people think she does."

"That is true."

"She told me she would attend Mass everyday and lift you up in prayer. Sometimes out loud, during prayers of the faithful. Sometimes in silence. But she never forgot you. She offered all her Communions for your healing."

"I love her very much," I said, pausing my footsteps to look out at the snowcapped peak, which served as a backdrop to a sloping meadow of purple and yellow wildflowers. "She has always been special. She hardly ever cried – even as a baby. She is a total optimist."

"That explains why she decided to do something. She knew it would work."

"She thought it would work. Optimists can be wrong."

"So can pessimists."

It really didn't surprise me that Katie has prayed so hard for me. It's the kind of person she is. She once told me that every time a lab result comes through at the medical lab where she works, she says a Hail Mary for the patient. She is keenly aware that someone's world is about to come crashing down around them. When she gets home at night, she prays a decade of the rosary for each patient whose test portends bad news. I always thought that spoke to her extreme kindness. How surprised these people would be to know a complete stranger cared enough to spend time praying for them.

"What an incredible place this is," Danny said, hands on his hips, staring at the view. I looked in the same direction he was looking, to see the splendor through his eyes. I was startled to feel his hands on my waist, pulling me close. I looked into his eyes.

"Have you cried, Beth?" he asked softly. "Have you cried for your baby?"

"No," I said, blankly, turning back toward the view.

"Never?"

"Never."

He hugged my head to his chest and I heard him speak inside himself with my one ear. "It's time, Beth. It's time to cry. No matter what the psychiatric community, the media, the clinic staff or the laws of the United States may say, you have suffered the loss of a child."

"I have suffered," I said, breaking from his embrace to bend down and tie my shoe.

"The loss of a child. You have suffered the loss of a child."

"But I chose it," I said, standing and returning my gaze to the view. "How can there be a loss if someone chooses it? The choice I made was the one carried out. What I chose to happen did happen. Most people would consider that a victory, not a cause for mourning."

"Is it? Then why are you not victorious?"

"I don't know. The guilt, I guess."

"No, it's not the guilt. You are guilty, yes, of believing a lie. It's the lie that robs millions of women of one of this world's greatest gifts. But you are not miserable simply because of guilt. You have suffered a loss." A kind of intensity I have never heard overtook Danny's voice. "You have lost a child. That is why you suffer."

I continued to stare at the mountain. "Are we going to Pinnacle Peak or not?" I asked.

Danny stared too. "A voice is heard in Ramah," he said, with minimal expression. "Mourning and great weeping, Rachel weeping for her children and refusing to be comforted, because her children are no more."

"And what is that?"

"Jeremiah 31:15. It's a verse I came across in post-abortion healing literature. I was irate when I first read it because it discounted the fathers. Don't fathers weep for their children too? I was quite certain I was the only one weeping for my child. I was quite certain her mother was not."

He unlocked his eyes from their distant stare and looked into mine. "Now," he said, "I'm not certain. Not at all."

"I know you want me to weep, Danny. I know you think that's cathartic. But it's just not what I do. I don't cry, Danny. It's kind of a genetic thing. Lovely women aren't big criers."

"Then, how do you mourn?"

"I don't know."

"Well, I do. You become a drug addict and then somehow miraculously part ways with your drugs, throw yourself into your school work, graduate summa cum laude, open an animal shelter, channel all of your compassion to the care of animals, refuse to marry and resolve to remain childless. You do all of this with a silent, clandestine ache inside that will neither subside, nor bring you to your knees so someone can come and render aid."

"What would you have me do, Danny? Sit in a corner and cry every day of my life? I could do that. But what good will that do? It won't change anything. It won't bring back my –" I stopped short of saying it. I couldn't say those two words together – *my* and *baby*.

"No, tears won't bring your baby back. But they will change something. They will change you. You can't properly mourn until you admit there was someone to mourn and that you have the right to mourn her."

"Do I? Do I have that right, Danny? What gives a killer the right to mourn the victim?"

"Because maybe there were two victims, Beth. Maybe when you're 14 years old, you're not fully aware of what you're doing. And maybe the people around you, telling you to do it, have something other than your best interest in mind."

He put his arms around me and we stood in silence for quite a few minutes.

"We better start making our way back, Danny. It's getting late."

"Yeah, you need to be in bed early tonight. I'm picking you up at 5:30, right?"

"Yeah, that should be fine," I said. "I don't have to check in until 7."

"Are you scared, Beth?"

"Petrified."

"You are doing an amazing thing."

"I just wish today was tomorrow and I had this whole thing behind me."

"Today will be tomorrow soon enough, Lovely lady. Don't worry. Everything will be fine."

It's not so much the procedure, but the hospital that terrifies me. Smooth, cold surfaces of steel and vinyl. Slick chrome handles on marbled grey Formica. Everything completely utilitarian and functional. Nothing for the purposes of warmth or beauty. Nothing to suggest that the place is about anything but getting the job done. Wires, tubes, probes, spiral cords, hanging on the walls as if they were great art. Why can't there be a painting of an ocean or a print of a hibiscus? Would those things diminish the quality of medical care? Would they lure the doctors into irresistible daydreams about distant tropical vacations, distracting them from life-saving procedures? Watercolor paintings of sand and foam serve no purpose in the business of keeping hearts pumping. So you will not find one in a hospital room.

I imagine what Thomas Jefferson might think if he came back from the dead and ended up in an examining room. I'm sure he'd assume he had been worm holed into a torture chamber. There are many frightening devices in a hospital for which the imagination invents uses even worse than what reality intended. The beautiful thing about modern medicine, though, is – as menacing as the machines look – they have taken the majority of pain and even discomfort out of treatment. I've seen enough cowboy movies to know that machines and hypodermics are preferable to whisky and a pocket knife if you find yourself needing a bullet removed, for instance. And dentistry before the modern age? Forget it. A world without Novocain is a scary place.

The dentist I visit regularly. But doctors I avoid. Lying on a table in the company of latex-gloved strangers takes me back to a place I don't want to be. But, to save a life. To save a life would be the only reason I would do it. That's how much I hate it.

Unfortunately, my niece's life depends on my torso being split open and my liver cut in two. I am donating half of it to her. A congenital metabolic condition has caused liver failure and a transplant is her only hope of survival. She doesn't have the luxury of time to wait for a deceased organ donor, so I am sharing my liver – nearly a perfect tissue match – with her.

It is scary on many levels. Of course, I'm afraid of all things medical. I'm afraid of physical suffering that goes with recovery. I'm afraid of the death that would accompany my failure to recover. But mostly, I'm afraid my niece will not survive. I've never been afraid for anyone else like I am for her.

My sister looked as if she hadn't slept in 102 years when she came into my room with a bouquet of peach colored roses. I smiled at her thoughtfulness. Not that she brought me roses, but that they were peach. I had once told her it was my favorite rose. I had told a lot of people this, mostly men that I had dated, and have always received red roses.

"Beth, you know I can never thank you enough," Laura said, taking my hand.

"I know," I said. "You don't need to. Just let me borrow your red cashmere sweater."

"How are you feeling?"

"Fine," I said. "How are you?"

She shook her head, and a look of grief washed across her face.

"Remember when we were kids and my diamond stud earrings that Grandma gave me disappeared? I blamed you for it."

"Yup. I took them," I said. "Hocked them to buy drugs."

"I didn't have any evidence, but I was so certain you had stolen them, I resolved that day never to give you anything ever again."

I smiled. "And I don't think you ever did. And I never gave you anything either. In fact, I took quite a few more things from you in addition to those earrings."

"And now, you are giving me something I never can repay you for."

I smiled and squeezed her hand. "Can we call it even, then?"

"What can I do for you, Beth?" she asked. "Just name it. What is it that you need or want?"

"I want Julie to live."

Doctors give her a 60 percent chance, based on the survival rates of other transplant recipients with her level of deterioration. As for me, the donor, they give me a 99.5 percent chance of making it.

"For once, we agree on something," Laura said with a sideways smile. She squeezed my hand tight and moved it from side to side, as one might congratulate someone on some kind of victory.

And with that, decades of sibling rivalry came to an abrupt halt and all that was left between us was an aching hope for a small child's future. From that moment forward, we started treating each other like two grown women, who met each other at the water cooler or at a PTA meeting, found something in common and built a casual but long-lasting friendship.

## 15

# Time Without Seasons

I awoke to someone's hand on my forehead. It was a warm hand, but I could not see who it belonged to because my eyes seemed to be taped shut. Why would they tape a liver donor's eyes shut, I wondered. I was finally able to muster enough power to foist my eyelids open with a few sharp blinks. Katie was smiling sweetly at me. I could not smile back. My face muscles would not respond. A sharp pain lay within and across my belly. I should have been happy to wake up alive because deep down I had wondered if I would. But the physical pain, the nausea and the six week recovery ahead of me crowded the joy right out. Dread clouded in.

"Hey, Sis," Katie said softly. "Hey, you did it."

"Julie?" It was all I could do to open my mouth and speak, even just one word.

"She's fine, Beth. She made it through fine. She's in recovery."

I closed my eyes and returned to sleep for what seemed like five or ten minutes. But when I opened my eyes again, Katie was gone and my mother was sitting in a chair next to me, holding my hand. My eyes felt lighter this time.

"Beautiful Beth," Mom said. "You did it. You saved a little girl's life. Again."

"Yes, if I ever go back to church," I said, "they're going to name me patron saint of livers." My words were slurred and muffled, as if I had pillow stuffing in my mouth.

Mom expelled a joyful laugh. I wanted to laugh, too, at my own cleverness, but my belly hurt too much.

"If you ever return to the Church," she grinned, "they're going to declare me patron saint of mothers whose incorrigible children return to the Faith in the nick of time, just before driving their mothers insane."

"Mom?"

"Yes, Honey?"

"What ever happened to Charlie?"

"Charlie?"

"The one you fostered. Charlie. Do you ever hear from her."

"Got a Christmas card from her last year. She is married with two little boys."

"So, do you think she found the best things?"

"I think the best things found her."

I dosed off again and awoke to the sound of crying. It was a newborn cry, thin and rhythmic. My feet touched the cold tiles and I wondered where my slippers were. It was like standing on a block of ice. I looked around the room, trying to locate the origin of the cries. I opened the hospital door and a torrent of yellow light poured over me. I stepped out into the warmth, onto an endless bed of soft grass – too soft to be grass, really, but that's what it was. The crying suddenly became louder, as if someone had removed ear plugs from my ears, and my biceps flexed with the instantaneous weight of the most beautiful creature I had ever seen. I looked into her eyes and said "shhhhh," as I bounced her lightly. She immediately quit crying and stared at me, at once bewildered and wise, with the soul of someone who understood many things that a baby cannot. I pressed her cheek to mine and gathered enough breath to utter, "Hello, beautiful." I felt an overwhelming current of affection course through me. I stayed lost in devotion for a length of time I cannot quantify – was it a minute or an hour or a day? Or maybe many days. It might have been years, except there was no passing of seasons. Nothing changed for the whole duration that I held her to my breasts and loved her with a love unsurpassed by any creature's love for another. And then, I awoke. This time, it was Danny sitting at my bedside.

"Hello, Lovely lady," he said, kissing me on the forehead.

I grabbed his shoulders with all the strength I could muster.

"Danny," I gasped. I wanted to tell him that I had held her. That God had let me hold my baby. That she is beautiful and perfect. But I couldn't tell him. To say those things would have been presuming to deserve it. And I would never be deserving of such a moment. And so, I resolved to think of her as a post-anesthesia dream. "Danny, I'm glad you're here."

ಶ್ರೀ ಶ್ರೀ ಶ್ರೀ ಶ್ರೀ ಶ್ರೀ

The following day, Dad and Danny set up camp in my hospital room, watching baseball until the nurse ordered me to walk a few laps around the hall. I asked if I could walk to Julie.

"Gives me more of an incentive than a trip to nowhere," I said.

"OK," the nurse said. "I'll follow you with the wheelchair. Just in case."

Danny took my arm and helped me to my feet and held it firm on the slow trek to the children's ward. Dad had the other arm.

Julie was surrounded by shiny, inflated Mylar and stuffed animals, which included a Dalmatian, a grey cat with white paws, a giraffe and a brown platypus that sported an orange ribbon around its neck. Mom and Laura were sitting in chairs by her bedside. Mom was reading letters from Julie's classmates. I was surprised by how good Julie looked. And when she saw me, it seemed to me like a rush of color washed into her face, and aside from the background of yellow still lingering in her complexion, she looked like a kid who hadn't been sick a day in her life.

"Aunt Beth! Grandpa! Danny!"

"Hi, Squirt," I said, hobbling over with my IV on wheels. "How's my partner?"

"Good," she said, grinning.

"You look gorgeous," Danny told her. Dad agreed.

"It's good to see you up and around," Laura said, standing to hug me. "They're making you walk, huh?"

"Yeah," I said. "Wild horses couldn't have kept me from coming down here to see this brave girl."

Julie beamed. "Thanks for saving my life, Aunt Beth. Let me know if you ever need an organ or anything. I'll give you something of mine."

She picked up a piece of paper that had been lying beside her on the bed. "Here," she said. "This is for you. I'm not quite finished with it, but you can look at it now."

It was a pencil drawing of me reaching over a cliff to save a little girl, who had fallen over the edge. Across the bottom, it read

*To Aunt Beth. The biggest hero in the world. I love you. Your niece and biggest fan, Julie.*

ಬ⚜ಛ⚜ಬ⚜ಛ⚜ಬ⚜ಛ⚜ಬ⚜ಛ

The organ donor foundation convinced me it would be a great help to humanity if I agreed to be interviewed for a national morning show. In the interest of raising awareness for this branch of medicine and increasing the pool of live organ donors, I agreed. And so, Julie and I appeared together as one of several pairs of people who were givers and recipients of life. The most interesting was the story of an American doctor who met an ailing 4-year-old boy while providing free medical care on a mission to Africa. The boy needed a liver, so the doctor flew him to Johns Hopkins Medical Center and gave him part of his. After having fully recovered, the boy was returned to his family, amidst tears and laughter and dancing and the kind of brightly-colored jubilation that overtakes entire villages.

Mom and Danny took turns taking care of me for the next three weeks. And three weeks short of the average recuperation rate, I felt my old self again. Julie continued to recover and thrive. Not too long after I was feeling better, she was out bike riding with her Dad. The human body is an incredible thing. Who would have thought one person's body could give another life? I guess that happens 200,000 times every day, in delivery rooms, rice fields and straw huts around the world, but it really drives the point home when you know that part of one of your vital organs ends up in someone else's belly.

Danny tried to use my so-called heroic deed to prove to me that my life has meaning, beyond what I had even understood. He also tried to use it as evidence that I would be willing to sacrifice my life for another. But I had only a half-percent chance of having to give my life for Julie. In the end, I really only sacrificed three weeks of my life for her. Would I have donated my liver to Julie if the odds were reversed and I had a 99.5 percent chance of dying?

"Odds aside, Beth, how many people are standing in line, offering up their livers?" Danny pointed out.

"Well, Mom would have done it, but she didn't match. Katie and Laura have children, so we wouldn't let them take the chance."

"No matter how ordinary you try to make it look, Beth, what you did is not something the average person signs up for. Why can't you just admit you are not the same person you once were, Beth?"

"Not the same person? I feel the same. I am who I've always been."

"You were addicted to drugs. And now you're not. You robbed your sister blind and now you're giving her your liver to save her child. Something brought you out of the abyss, Beth. What was it?"

"The unconditional love of my parents. Prescription medications to treat my depression. Lots of counseling."

"Yeah, counseling," he said. "But they never addressed the abortion?"

"I never told them. I've never told a single soul besides you."

"You are in the final stages, Beth. You are just steps short of finishing a marathon. Do you want to finish?"

I wrinkled my forehead at him. "Plain English, please, coach. What are you talking about?"

"OK, this is what I want you to do, Beth. You may not want to do it, but you're going to have to if you want to be through with this albatross you've worn around your neck for the majority of your life."

"What? What do I need to do?"

"Give your child a name. And go to Confession."

"No. I can't do that."

"Which part?"

"Either."

"Beth, you've got to face your grief. You can't pretend any more there is nothing to grieve. You know it's not nothing. If it were, it wouldn't have followed you and beat you down all these years. Come here, I want to show you something."

He took my hand, led me to the computer and started typing.

A website for the National Memorial for the Unborn in Chattanooga, Tennessee, popped up. Danny pulled me onto his lap. Engraved messages from parents to their deceased unborn children filled a marble wall.

*I knew too late I loved you. I'll hold you in Heaven. Mommy*
*Forgive me for I knew not what I was doing.*
*The joy of "you" I will not know.*
*I knew the truth too late.*
*Forever in our hearts. Your loving Grandma and Grandpa*
*Psalm 27:10*
*Lost May 1994. Daddy does love you.*
*Forgive us, Father*
*If I knew then what I know now…*

*May 1974: Now the healing begins*
*I long to nurture you.*
*We love and miss you. Your brother and his Mommy.*
*If only I knew... Mom.*
*Two of God's Little Ones, entrusted to me, forgive me.*
*Then, I didn't know I loved you. Now, I will never forget.*
Love, Mommy.

Danny talked softly into my ear. "See, Beth? You are not alone. Your grief is real. Look how many others feel it? Could all of these people be crazy or is there just even a small chance that you are entitled to feel the pain of loss?"

"Yes," I said. "It's real. It's very really."

"Then, give your child a place on this memorial."

"These people have already said it all," I said. "What more is there for me to say?"

"Their words are for their children, Beth. You have words of your own. For your own."

I closed my eyes and tipped my head back onto Danny's shoulder. "You know, sometimes, when I'm watching my nieces and nephews bouncing on Mom's trampoline, I see her. I see her like a phantom, jumping there too. Smiling, giggling, holding hands with her cousins as they bounce themselves into frantic joy, while my Mom watches with a broad smile, sitting in her chaise lounge with her wide brimmed hat, sipping a lemonade. Then the little girl -- her smile fades and she stops jumping and just stands there on the trampoline, in a daze, staring, while all the other children bounce around her. And then, she just fades away. And I feel so bad for my mother, whom I robbed of a grandchild. And I feel bad for my child, who never got to be loved by my mother. My mother is pure love to her grandchildren. She would have made my child so happy."

"Yes," Danny said.

"You know, she would be older now than I was on the day of the abortion. But I always still think of her as a little girl. Always."

"A little you."

"Yeah."

"Very beautiful."

"Maybe beautiful to the caliber of Katie."

"I've always pictured my baby as a girl too," Danny said. "I don't know why."

Danny typed "Hope Celeste" into the search field of the Memorial's virtual wall.

*Hope Celeste. My heart holds what my arms never will. Love, Daddy.*

I burst into tears, and Danny turned my face into his flannel shirt.

"I'm sorry, Danny," I said. "I'm sorry for your loss."

"And I'm sorry for yours," he said, holding my head tight against his chest until I had doused his shirt for several minutes.

Danny stroked my hair and waited for the torrent of tears to subside. Then he picked up my chin with his forefinger and kissed me tenderly on the lips. A deeper kiss followed.

At that moment, I knew I wanted to give myself entirely to this man, spend every day of the rest of my life with him and die in his arms. Or, if I could have just skipped to the last part, at that moment, I would have done so.

# 16

# Firefly Walls

I was excited to see a returned e-mail from my friend Rebecca. It had been several weeks and I had just assumed that, for some reason, my message hadn't reached her.

*Dear Beth,*

*I was delighted to hear from you. I have thought of you so often throughout the years. How is your family? How is your Aunt Lily. I have such fond memories of spending Thanksgivings at your folks' house. Remember the gobbling contest your Dad hosted for all us fools? No one could out-gobble your Aunt Lily. I would love to see her again. My youngest daughter, who is now 6, was born with Down Syndrome. It really helped a lot that I had known your aunt. Because of all the fun we had together, I was not tempted to despair. Jeffrey really wanted to terminate the pregnancy when the amnio results came in. It was very difficult to stand up to the pressure, not just from within my own home, but from friends and doctors as well. Had I not known Lily, I would have most likely agreed with all of them. And then I would have had that to live with the rest of my life. I don't know if I could have endured it, even though the arguments for termination are so sound. There are times when we cannot live on practicalities alone and we must employ our intuition, protecting and nurturing what lies within us, be it perfect or flawed. The differences between Jeffrey and me on this issue nearly de-stroyed our marriage, but he came to accept my decision as he began to understand my love for your Aunt Lily. I still have a picture of me and Lily, smiling and hugging in a giant leaf pile, leaves strewn in our hair like parade confetti. Please tell her how important she is to me and my family, would you?*

*My daughter, Mabel, is gorgeous, as you can see from the photo. And I don't know what we would do without her. Notice the impish smile and you will surmise that she is quite the comic and brings more than our fair share of laughter to our lives. She is pictured with her sister Monica, who is 10, and brother Robert, who is 13. They are both very good students and kind individuals.*

*Are you still in Washington? We are in Fort Lauderdale now. We moved to Florida to be with my mother after my father died three years ago. We have a small ranch with a boarding stable and a couple of horses of our own. I work part time at my children's school. On weekends you will find us horseback riding on the beach. Mabel struggles with her speech, but "neigh" was her third word, right after "Mommy" and "Daddy."*

*Tell me, what marvelous events have occurred in your life? I know there must be many. You were always so talented and beautiful. I am so glad we re-established contact. If you can manage a trip to Florida, it would be such a joy to see you. I would love for Aunt Lily and Mabel to meet.*

*And yes, I do remember Professor Snell. Remember how we all talked about chipping in and getting him a Men's Wearhouse gift card?*

*Take care,*
*Rebecca*


*Dear Rebecca,*
*Congratulations on your beautiful children. Yes, I can see Mabel is quite the character. She is beautiful. I am so glad you stood firm on your decision. I am sure she will bring many people great joy, just like Lily.*

*I am sorry to have to tell you that Lily passed away this past spring. She had a stroke and lived for quite some time in a vegetative state. I still remember the last lucid day we had together. She told me she wanted to visit her late husband's grave. She was going to take his favorite lunch – Bacon cheeseburger and fries – and have a picnic with him.*

*You are right when you say Mabel will change many lives. Lily certainly did. So many people testified to that at her funeral.*

*One of my favorites came from my niece, Olivia, who said, "Other grown-ups always say they're going to play with you later. But they never do. They're too busy doing important stuff. But not Lily. She thought playing with me was the important stuff."*

*You're probably wondering if I have any children. I don't. I never married. I run a couple of animal shelters, and in my spare time, I paint. I had been taking care of Lily, but now I live by myself in Seattle, not too far from Mom and Dad, who are doing great. They are still fostering.*

*I would love to come out for a visit. Or have your family come this way. Mom has plenty of room for guests, as you probably remember.*

*If you get a chance, could you send me a copy of that photograph of you and Lily? You have no idea how much I miss her.*

*Also, please send your mailing address. I have something I'd like to send to Mabel.*

*Talk to you soon,*
*Beth*

I actually wasn't sure what I was going to send to Mabel. But I knew I wanted to give her something of Lily's. Mom has all the stuff from Lily's childhood packed away in her attic. Someday soon, I would go look through it.

ಬ⚹ଓ⚹ಬ⚹ଓ⚹ಬ⚹ଓ⚹ಬ⚹ଓ⚹

We had told John about Agnes when he was a child, and she had come to him many times in his dreams, sometimes to play ring around the rosie with him, sometimes to hold his hand and walk him through a dark forest, sometimes to give him a lime-flavored snow cone when he was hot and thirsty or cover him with a tartan blanket when he was cold. Agnes was Auntie Bev's best friend in the nursing home and the one who had appeared to Mom in a dream during the time she was struggling with infertility to let her know she would have a baby boy. That baby boy turned out to be John, and, for whatever reason, she made her presence known to him throughout his childhood. After he entered the teen years, he never saw her again. Until last night.

Katie called to give me the news. She had called John to see how he was settling into his new dorm.

"He told me he had just met his roommate and was getting things put away. He said he laid down for a minute to test out his new bed and he dosed off. And you remember Agnes?"

"Uh-huh?"

"She was with this very pretty young woman -- about college aged – and a little girl about five years old. The young woman said, *Seek mercy. Tell your sister.* John didn't know who she had meant it for – you, me or Laura. But he said she looked just like me when I was that age."

"Yes," I said, "I think it was meant for me." I could barely get the words out, I was so stunned.

"Oh, OK," she said, "because Laura had no idea what it meant. So, what does it mean?"

"I may be able to tell you someday, Katie, but not today. It's a very long story and I've got to get over to the animal shelter."

Yes, I knew immediately what it meant. My daughter had come to me with a message. Just like Jolene's daughter had come to her. Jolene's daughter had meant to use those two words to save her mother from the guilt of her past. My daughter, I was certain, had meant to do the same for me. But neither daughter gave a shred of detail on exactly how one should go about this. What exactly is mercy and where do you find it?

These were the thoughts that occupied my mind as I drifted off to sleep past midnight. A half hour later I awoke startled with this answer: "It's not a what, it's a who. Mercy has a name."

I tried in vain for more than an hour to go back to sleep. Then, I got up and went into my studio, turned on Vivaldi's *Four Seasons, Spring Allegro*, and set a canvas on my easel for the first time since losing Lily. I knew, when this painting was finished, it would be Danny's.

A couple hours later, I could hardly make another brush stroke, so I decided to return to bed. I put my paintbrush down, stretched and turned out the light. On the way past my desk, I picked up the relic Pablo had wanted to give Lily, as was my nightly habit ever since I unpacked it from that box. For me, it is an eternal link between Pablo and Lily – and me and them. I pressed it into my palm, hoping to press some essence of the two of them into my being. I imagined that the tiny case housing the saint's bone fragment had left a flower-shaped impression in my palm, though I couldn't see it in the dark. I wondered if Pablo might still have the opportunity to introduce Lily to St. Toribio Romo. Maybe he already did. The three of them might have been having a nice chat, even at that very moment.

I jumped when my e-mail chimed. I was 90 percent certain it was middle-of-the-night spam, but I leaned over my computer to check anyway. It was an urgent notice from AlwaysInStock.com, telling me I had only two days left to take advantage of free shipping.

My eyes fell on an icon of the National Memorial for the Unborn that Danny had left on my computer desktop. I clicked. "Add name to virtual wall" popped up. I sat down, rested my fingers on the keyboard and waited. After several minutes, my fingers began to move.

*Katherine Therese. Time passes. Mercy heals. But you will never be forgotten.*

I put my head on my desk and wept.

I was awakened in the soft dawn by the phone, my eyes sticky and swollen with uncried tears, penned in by eyelids too heavy to withstand the exhaustion, though there was an abundance of unfinished sorrow that still needed to cascade past them.

I had told the nursing home to call us when Jolene passed away, assuming we were probably the only next of kin. So when caller ID registered Garden Grove Nursing Home, I thought we were headed to yet another funeral. But the voice on the other end was Jolene's.

"Tell your mother thanks for sending her priest friend to see me."

"Her priest friend?"

"Father Tomas. I ain't Catholic but it was nice to have someone to talk to."

"Oh, OK," I said. "I'll tell her."

"How is Therese?"

"She's fine. She goes by Terry, you know."

"And I go by Jo."

"Jo. You never told me."

"You makin' any more trips to Burbank?"

"I have none planned," I said. "Our friend who lived there passed away."

"Oh, I see."

"Why do you ask?"

"I thought maybe I'd see you again before I die."

"Well," I said, trying to ignore the knot that was forming in my stomach. "Maybe I can come some day."

"You should do that, Beth. You and me, we got a lot in common."

"We do?"

"We're both alone. You, at least you have your animals. I got nobody."

"I know, Jo."

"I used to think that was OK. When I was your age. To have no one to answer to. I thought that was the good life. But when you're old and lonely, there ain't no good in that. There's just one miserable day after another until the day you die. And on that day, you die alone."

"Call Father Tomas," I said. "I'm sure he'll come and see you again."

After I hung up, the rest of my tears were able to escape in one steady, flowing, seemingly eternal stream.

ಬಿ✗ಣ✗ಬಿ✗ಣ✗ಬಿ✗ಣ✗ಬಿ✗ಣ

I decided I had lived with my walls long enough. Mom said she would help me redecorate with an eye towards happiness, such as we found in the vibrant mismatched decor of Pablo's little house on Orange Street. With each swipe of the paint roller, my house became less Swan Sea and more Firefly. And I became more at home with the color yellow and the notion of hope.

I bought a Terra-cotta colored slipcover for my sofa and draped it with Pablo's quilt. Mom offered me free access to her accumulation of forgotten knick knacks, which she stores in her attic. I needed to visit the attic anyway to find something of Lily's to send to Mabel.

I love Mom's attic. I call it Mom's attic because there is not one single thing in there that belongs to Dad. Attics are meant largely for useless items belonging to women. Dads store the things they never use in basements: sports equipment, barbeque utensils, coffee table books about hunting and boxed collector's sets of documentaries on war and nature – all received over a lifetime of Father's Days.

The thing I love most about Mom's attic is the smell -- hot wood mixed with aging fabrics, permeated with dust and humidity.

I found several things that would look good in my place, including a tiffany lamp that no longer worked, a couple of candle wall sconces and an Our Lady of Guadalupe tapestry.

There were many boxes with Lily's name – probably close to a dozen – things she left behind when she moved in with me. I chose the one marked "Lily's toys." I slit it open. Mom reached in and rescued Red Rabbit, which had been wedged between the plastic arm of a baby doll and a purple Magna Doodle.

A smile crept across Mom's face. "This was not only Lily's favorite toy, but Pablo Puppy's too, remember?" she said. "There were a number of showdowns over this thing."

"I thought it was Laura's."

"It was. Her secret admirer sent it to her, remember?"

"Oh, yeah. Good ol' Uncle Jimmy. How did Lily get it?"

"Laura gave it to her when Lily was feeling sad at not having a boyfriend on Valentine's Day."

I took Red Rabbit and looked into his face. He was worn – matted and misshapen – but still happy. "I don't think we can part with this," I said, squeezing his middle, so his large feet flew up towards his belly. "I think Laura may want it back."

I decided to send Mabel Lily's favorite doll. Her rubbery cheeks were stained yellow-orange from something Lily had tried to feed her.

"What did Lily call her?" I asked.

"Just 'Baby.'"

"Oh, yeah. Do you think Mabel will mind that her face is stained?"

"I know Lily wouldn't have."

"Look, we could send her this." I pulled out a purple purse embroidered with Disney princesses and a set of fake car keys inside.

"Nah. I think Baby is better. More personal."

"I just hope Mabel knows what to feed her."

"I don't think she's too finicky. One time Lily fed her three-month-old rotten Easter eggs recovered from under a bush in the back yard. Baby didn't flinch."

"Are there any clothes?"

Mom shook her head. "You know how Lily was."

"Maybe Mabel will like naked babies too."

Mom smiled. "I'll give you a receiving blanket for her."

"Mom, what's in here?" It was a cedar trunk.

"Those are all the things the moths are not allowed to touch."

"May I?" I said raising the lid. "I'm not a moth."

"Sure. There's nothing for decorating in there, but you can look."

"Which one of us wore this?" I asked, holding up a white organza dress with a high bodice and pearls sewn on in the shape of flowers.

"That's Lily's First Communion dress," Mom said. "And yours and Laura's and then Katie's. Isn't it beautiful?"

"It is," I said. "I have no memory of wearing this."

"You don't remember your First Communion?"

"No, do you remember yours?"

"Vaguely. But I remember Lily's perfectly. On the way back to her seat from the Communion line, she had this huge smile on her face and she clapped her hands quietly and whispered, 'Yay!'"

Mom took the dress from me gently and held it up before her. "I remember her in this dress like it was yesterday. I think the next time I saw that caliber of joy on her face was on her wedding day."

Frank burst into tears at the sight of Lily, coming down the aisle, in that gorgeous, flowing white dress. Lily picked that dress because it had more fabric than any other. You could have probably made seven dresses out of that one. Lily said it looked like Cinderella's ball gown. She looked very hard to find clear pumps, but we were unable to find anything that looked like a glass slipper to fit Lily's very wide foot. She was not dismayed.

"That O.K.," she said. "My Prince Charming already know where I live."

Frank was apparently very happy with Lily's choice of attire.

"Lily is so pretty, I cry," Frank would later tell a reporter.

A story came out about Frank and Lily's marriage on their one-year anniversary. The reporter asked them if they ever fight. "Why would we fight?" Lily said. "We love each other."

Frank added, "People who love each other make each other happy. That's what it means to be married."

When the reporter asked their secret to making each other happy, Lily said, "I fill up his heart. He fill up my heart. When I sad, he make me happy. When he sad, I make him happy."

"We dance together every night," Frank said. "Lily loves to dance. And I bring her flowers. Sometimes after work, I bring them home."

"And what do you do to make Frank happy, Lily?" the reporter asked.

"I laugh at his jokes. He like to hear me laugh. And I tell him he is handsome. I tell him from my heart, because he the most handsome man I ever seen."

"And she cook me dinner every night," Frank said. "I like her meatloaf best. But her spaghetti good too. But messy."

When asked if they want to have children, Lily said, "Oh, yes. We love babies."

"If God wants to send us a baby, He can send us a baby," Frank said. "But He probably won't because my wife and me both got Down Syndrome and He doesn't send babies to lots of people with Down Syndrome. But that's OK if He doesn't. He gave me Lily. That's enough to make me happy for forever."

By the time the interview was over, the reporter was in tears. She took with her a copy of a photograph of Frank and Lily in front of the altar with Father Fitz. That photo appeared with the story, under the headline: *Down Syndrome Couple Discover True Love.*

Of course, the real test came when Frank got sick. Toward the end, he didn't know who anyone was, and he was often irritable and sometimes even downright belligerent.

"His brain is sick," Lily would explain. "His heart the same, but his brain is sick."

But there were times when the only consolation he had was Lily's presence. She could make him smile when no one else could. It was a simple technique, but it only worked for her. She would poke him in the ribs and make a face.

ಞ⚇ಡಞ⚇ಡ⚇ಞ⚇ಡ⚇ಞ⚇ಡ

When I got home from Mom's house, I swaddled Baby, placed her in a Fed Ex flat rate box and enclosed a note.

*Dear Mabel,*
*I am a friend of your Mommy's and I wanted to send you a present. This doll belonged to my Aunt Lily. She was special like you. This was her favorite doll. She got it when she was your age and loved it for many years to come. I hope you like babies.*
*Love from far away in Seattle,*
*Beth*

Less than a week later, I got an e-mail from Rebecca, telling me how much Mabel loves the doll. She named her Lily. Rebecca bought the doll a wardrobe of clothes, but Mabel refuses to put any of them on, preferring her baby in the buff.

Rebecca attached two photos: one of Mabel hugging Baby and one of Lily and Rebecca, with leaf-strewn hair, smiling at the camera from the middle of a huge pile of leaves. Rebecca is giving the camera a thumbs up as Lily squeezes her around the middle. I remember the discomfort associated with Lily's devotion. She had such strong affection, it was often difficult to breathe, if you happened to be its object.   How I miss that pain.

# 17

## All the Way Through

I had told no one this. But about three weeks after Gregory Hill interviewed me for the organ donor story, he called.

"Just wanted to follow-up, with you," he said in his velvety voice. "See how you are feeling. Are you recovering well?"

"Very well, thank you," I said. "It's nice of you to check in."

"And your adorable niece? How is she?"

"Fantastic. Better than ever."

"Glad to hear it. The story is set to air Friday."

"Oh, great," I said. "Thanks for calling to let me know."

"Well, to be honest," he said, "I had other reasons for calling."

"Which are?"

"Well, it would be improper for me to tell you, so before the story is all said and done, but after Friday I will be ethically at liberty to call and tell you that I haven't been able to stop thinking about you since I met you."

"Really? Why?" I tried to hide the surge of excitement that coursed through me at the thought of someone like Gregory Hill showing an interest in me.

"Well, I can't tell you. It sounds too cliché. And you might laugh at me. And I can't bear to have the most beautiful woman I've ever met laugh at me."

He was right. It was cliché. I had heard the "most beautiful woman" line on quite a few occasions. All the Lovely women have.

"Oh, I won't laugh at you," I said.

"So, I have your promise on that, Beth? If I call you up Friday after the story airs and tell you you're the most beautiful woman I've ever met and ask if I can fly out and take you to dinner, you will *not* laugh at me?"

"No," I said, smiling.

"No, you don't promise, or no, you won't laugh?"

"I'm not going to answer that. You'll just have to take your chances."

I watched Gregory Hill on TV for the next three mornings. I thought of what it might be like to be his lover. I am sure many women imagine it, but I had actually been given a remote shot at it – at least in theory.

Gregory Hill is intelligent and accomplished. He has a voice made for audio and a face made for the camera. He is famous and well off. Yet, by virtue of his media career – the places he goes and the people he meets -- he deals with life at a depth most people never reach. He comes across on camera and in person as compassionate and involved. I surmised that it might be outright idyllic to be loved by Gregory Hill. For three days, I more than imagined it. I contemplated it.

He called on Friday, a half hour after the story aired. I hung up with Mom to take his call. He wanted to know what I thought of the story, how I was feeling, how Julie is doing and where I might like to go for dinner. We arranged to meet at the Space Needle and would decide from there where to eat. I can't tell you how many dates have originated in the shadow of the Space Needle. Not a small number of them have been mine. But the one with Gregory Hill felt different, like something new was afoot. It had been a long time since I had a date. My recent years had been occupied. With Lily. With Danny. With Pablo. With death. With grief. With illness. It felt as if I were climbing out of a cave. Except for one thing. Emerging from a cave, you would expect to see daylight, but Gregory Hill's plane did not touch down until 8:45, well after the sun had set.

We decided to get a bite at the Space Needle Restaurant. We talked about the view, what it was like to grow up in Seattle, what it was like to grow up in L.A. I am the oldest of four. He is the youngest of three. I could have guessed he was the baby of the family, I told him.

"Why is that?" he asked.

"You enjoy life. No worries. Am I right?"

I told him I am not complaining about my upbringing, but that wasn't true. Every eldest child lodges complaints about the inequity of birth order. The oldest child in the family never enjoys the same carefree existence as the youngest. This is because new parents are neurotic lunatics, and seasoned parents are tired lunatics. When you are a new parent, every small and large thing is viewed as a large thing. This is why I was never allowed to eat a donut in the grocery cart. It was too sticky, too sugary, too fatty, too crumbly and it would set a bad precedent for wanting a donut every time we went to the store. Seasoned parents are too tired to tell the child that the donut is too sticky, too sugary, too fatty and too crumbly and will set a bad precedent. So the seasoned parent gives the child the donut and enjoys a messy, but peaceful shopping trip. I got the idea of wanting a donut in a shopping cart from another kid I saw enjoying a pink frosted jelly-filled with sprinkles. Her face looked like a battlefield. I couldn't figure out why *her* mother didn't notice that the donut was too sticky, too sugary, too fatty and too crumbly. What I didn't know at the time was that the little girl had older siblings who were at school, putting her in the proper birth order to get a donut while grocery shopping.

I remember John sitting up in the grocery cart, holding an entire loaf of French bread and gnawing on it like a beaver chewing a log. Another shopper passing by chuckled and said, "I've never seen *that* before."

"What?" Mom said, gleefully. "A baby eating bread?"

"No," the woman said. "A baby eating the entire loaf."

John ended up with the whole loaf because he said, "bread," in his adorable little toddler boy voice when Mom placed it into the cart. And since Mom's germ phobia made it unthinkable for her to touch the bread with unclean hands, she couldn't just pinch off a piece for him. So she gave him the entire thing. John's hands were, of course, acceptably clean for touching the bread because they hadn't been allowed to handle anything but the grocery cart cover Mom brought with her on every shopping trip. Mom knew of the microscopic dangers that lurked in the grocery store because she had been told by a pediatrician once that the grocery store is the one place people are sure to go even when they are sick. Mom always got nervous when we got close to the cold and flu remedies or the chicken soup aisle.

I have vivid memories of being in the grocery cart and asking for bread when I was a little kid and I was told I had to wait until I got home.

"We need to pay for it first," Mom would say. "Besides, my hands aren't clean, so I can't break off a piece for you right now."

This sounded logical to me, but I threw a fit anyway. Toddlers are not interested in logic. They are interested in bread. Besides, it wasn't like I was asking for a pink-frosted jelly-filled donut with sprinkles.

Gregory Hill laughed heartily at all my insights. After dessert – a shared piece of Tiramisu cheesecake – he told me he was having too good a time to let the evening end. He suggested we head over to his hotel for a drink in the lounge, where he slid in next to me in a booth overlooking an indoor fountain composed of four spitting fish.

"So, you never did tell me," he said, swirling the ice in his White Russian. "Are you enjoying your celebrity since the story ran?"

"I've heard from quite a few people, including my third grade teacher. And all of Julie's classmates are asking her for autographs."

"She's a real sweetheart."

"Yeah, and that little boy from Africa, he was adorable."

"Yeah, a really cute kid. The kind that makes you almost consider having a few of your own."

"You don't have any children?"

"No, never been married. You?"

"No."

"I just couldn't imagine having kids with my lifestyle. I'm never home. It just wouldn't be fair to a wife or kids."

"So you're the perpetual bachelor."

"I guess so. At least for the foreseeable future."

"You're probably too busy to get lonely," I said, sipping my Irish coffee.

"Well, you don't have to be alone, just because you're single. You can still share special moments with a special someone." He slid in even closer to me and kissed me softly on the lips. I wanted his lips to linger on mine, and he knew it. "You have to find that special someone, though." He kissed me lightly again. "And that is never easy." He pressed his lips firmly on mine now and pulled me in tight to him. "If you want to ask me my opinion, I will tell you. I think I found her."

My heart was pounding.

"And you know what?" He picked my hand up in his. I wondered how his hands could be so warm after holding a cold drink. "I don't have to be home until 4 a.m. Monday morning. And I want to spend every moment until then with you." He punctuated his sentences with warm kisses on my hand, which he gazed at as if it were a found treasure. "And next weekend. And the one after that." He softly entwined his fingers with the hair on the back of my head and kissed me deeply.

"So, you're asking me to spend the night with you?"

"I don't mean to offend you, Beth. And I don't want you to think I'm a jerk. But I am incredibly attracted to you. Your beauty, yes. That's obvious. You're gorgeous. But you are just as beautiful on the inside, Beth. And I feel like I've known you for such a long time."

"But you haven't. And you don't. You don't know me at all." It took all the strength I had to get to my feet. I felt clumsy and awkward, as if all the blood had gone to my head, depriving my legs of whatever fuel they needed to function. I struggled to steady my high-heeled silver sandals. "Thank you for a wonderful evening, Gregory."

He stood up and took my hand. "Beth, wait, I'm sorry. I didn't mean to come on so strong. Let's just slow things down. We don't need to rush into anything. You set the pace, Beth. It'll be all on your timeline."

"What will be on my timeline? Exactly what?"

Gregory Hill took a deep breath and thought for a second. The question had left us with nothing but vacant space between us. He clearly did not have the answer.

⊗⭍⭏⭍⊗⭍⭏⭍⊗⭍⭏⭍⊗⭍⭏⭍⊗⭍⭏⭍

Frannie is out for a visit because she needed to get away after the death of her husband, Louis. I remember her from when we lived in Minneapolis. As a kid, I thought she was something special – a stylish dresser, fun and current in all her jargon. But by the time I was 16, I had her pegged as friendly and shallow. I made that assessment when we went back to Minneapolis for Grandpa's funeral. She was still married to her first husband then, but he didn't come with her. Frannie divorced him soon after to marry Louis.

I still can't figure out how she and Mom came to be best friends. They don't seem to have much in common. They see life through different lenses. Mom said that wasn't always the case. I assumed that meant that Frannie must have changed quite a bit since they had first met, but Mom told me it wasn't Frannie who had done the changing.

Everyone who knows Mom well knows it was John who changed her. Nobody exactly knows why or how, but everyone knows when. It was at 3:16 p.m. March 11, when John Jacob Lovely came barreling into the world, the time on his birth certificate reflecting the world's most popular Bible Scripture, marking him as something special in God's plans. "For God so loved the world..."

Mom brought Frannie over to see the animal shelter and then we all had an early dinner together on my back porch. We unwrapped the crinkly marigold-colored sandwich paper from our long, fat cold cut subs and passed around a liter of beer, pouring it into frosted mugs I store in my freezer for rare instances of company. The conversation was not dull. But it was somewhat depressing. What I gleaned was this:

Frannie, at the age of 58, is alone and lonely. Her two children have decided to remain childless, so there will be no grandchildren. The daughter is divorced and the son married. They spend holidays with their Dad. They phone her from his house. They have not forgiven her for cheating on him. She does not plan to ask them for forgiveness. They should not be so quick to judge, she says. They, after all, have not walked a mile in her three-inch heels.

But no one ought to feel sorry for her, she insists. She is alone by her own choice. She could have re-remarried. She had an offer after Louis died, but turned it down. It was too soon after his death. And besides, Robert just isn't right for her. She knows that because she was good friends with his late wife, Judy.

Frannie and Louis met Judy and Robert at a cancer support group. Louis was losing his battle with prostate cancer and Judy was in the final stages of colon cancer. When the couples had first met, Frannie had fantasized about someday being with Robert. He seemed so caring toward his ailing wife. She was able to fantasize about another man, while her husband was not yet dead, because the fire between her and Louis had gone out long ago. There wasn't even a glowing ember. But she stayed, of course, because Louis needed her. What kind of woman would leave a dying man?

Over the course of the eight months that the couples knew each other, they had dinner together at least once a week. They were the kind of evenings where the women would kick off their Aerosoles and tuck their stocking feet under their long flowing skirts, leaning into velour throw pillows on an over-stuffed sofa, large clusters of inferior-grade diamonds on their ring fingers, a glass of chardonnay or a margarita raised to their lips. The men would sit out on the patio drinking beer, watching the meat grill. Every now and again, when they all four convened for the meal, a glance, gilded in silence, would pass between Frannie and Robert. Neither one of them was sure what it meant, if anything. Frannie had hoped that it meant something. As time went on, however, the women became closer friends, and Judy revealed more and more of Robert's faults.

"I often wonder," Frannie mused, rubbing her finger around the rim of her beer mug, "if Judy suspected there was something between me and Robert and she was doing me a favor. Trying to save me. If so, I am grateful. She was a good friend."

"Maybe she just didn't want anyone else to have him," I said. "Maybe she made it all up."

"Hmmm," she said, taking a gulp of her beer. "I hadn't considered that."

Judy died in January, preceding Louis in death by just under three months. In that time, Robert did all he could to help Frannie, even caring for Louis when she had to be away for errands and offering solid advice on hospice, estate planning and DNRs.

"I actually don't know how I would have made it through without Robert," Frannie said.

About six weeks after Louis passed, Robert took Frannie in his arms and buckled her knees with a long, passionate kiss. They had been through so much together, he told her. He couldn't bear to be without her now.

"Apparently, men do not trash talk their wives the way women do their husbands," Frannie told us, "because Robert seemed to be completely unaware of all my shortcomings. All those evenings, poking at beef with their long forks in the back yard. Louis and Robert must have truly just talked about sports."

"Or Robert's eyes are completely open, and he loves you anyway," I said.

Frannie looked at Mom and grinned. "You've raised quite the romantic," she said. Then she looked at me. "So much like your mother. So much like her."

"Me romantic?" Mom said.

"Oh, yes. You forget I was there when you first met Jacob. You were head over heels, like I've never seen anyone in my life. And him too. And now look at you, Terry. Your house bursting at the seams with children and your children's children. I doubt there's much time for romance, though you've got quite a charming and handsome husband on your hands still. The day you first introduced him to me, I thought he was one of the most handsome men I'd ever seen. And he still is, even all these many years later." She took a sip and looked at me.

"And you, Beth. You have inherited the striking good looks of both your parents."

"Thank you," I said.

"You know, Frannie, it wasn't beauty that kept Jake and me together," Mom said. "It was truth."

"What truth?" Frannie said, with a coy smile.

"Quid est veritas," Mom said. I knew she was referring to Pontius Pilate's question to Jesus. But I knew Frannie would not know that. She was not home schooled by my mother, as I was in my junior and senior years.

"What?"

"Never mind." Mom contemplated her drink for a minute, rubbing her finger on the outside, wiping away the glass sweat as she went. "There was a time when I thought that I would not be growing old with Jake. It just seemed we had become strangers, and I didn't want to live with a stranger. And then, because of Lily, many things began to change. Jake didn't change. But my understanding of him did. The sacrifices he made for her made me realize what an unselfish person he is. At the same time, I began to realize what a selfish person I am. The light of truth, shed on those two facts, made me understand that I should want to stay forever. So I did."

"With no regrets," Frannie said.

"None," said Mom, taking a sip of her beer. "I once had a vision. At Katie's wedding. It was the one and only vision I ever had. Katie had chosen the most beautiful song for the wedding procession. Do you remember, Beth?"

It had made such a huge impression on me, I sang it for weeks inside my head, even against my own will.

*I will weep when you are weeping*
*When you laugh I'll laugh with you*
*I will share your joy and sorrow*
*Til we see this journey through*
*When we sing to God in Heaven*
*We shall find such harmony*
*Born of all we've known together*
*Of Christ's love and agony.*

Ah, yes. I remember. *The Servant Song.*

"As I heard that beautiful song, I had this vision," Mom said. "Of me at my life's end and Jake by my side, kneeling be-side my bed, holding my hand, smiling into my eyes, calming my fears. And I saw, enwrapped in that moment, many other moments too numerous to count. The preparing of food, the fluffing of pillows, the wringing out of wash clothes, the pushing of a wheelchair, the rubbing of swollen feet, the stroking of hair when tears are rolling. And I realized it may be me who ends up doing those things for him, or him for me. But in the end, what matters is that we saw the journey through. All the way through."

We all sat in silence for a few moments. I was trying to get over the shock of hearing my mother say she had contemplated leaving my father. I had never thought of that as a possibility. Their marriage wasn't perfect, especially in my younger years. It lacked warmth and depth. But I never considered the idea that it could end. The idea frightened me, even now. Even now when it has no possibility, and even now when I wouldn't have to wonder which parent I will live with and which one will have me on alternating weekends. I pushed the horrible idea out of my head.

"So, what exactly was wrong with Robert?" I asked Frannie. "According to Judy."

"He is hard-headed, possessive and terribly jealous," Frannie said. "Judy lived her life in a virtual prison, walking on eggs, trying not to upset him. She told me he felt more like a jailer to her than a friend."

"And you would never have picked up on that?"

"Never," she said. "And that's the scary thing. I happen to have pretty good intuition and I would have never suspected he was anything short of the perfect spouse."

"There is no such thing as the perfect spouse," Mom said.

"You know, come to think of it, I don't have great intuition," Frannie said, pointing a finger and looking up into the air at nothing in particular. "I would have never expected Louis to be the type to cheat on me."

"And he did?" I asked.

"Yup."

"Now why would that surprise you, Frannie?" Mom asked. "After all, he cheated with *you*."

"No, he never cheated on his first wife. He was divorced before we got together."

"But you weren't," Mom said.

"My marriage to Brad was, for all intents and purposes, over by the time I met Louis. And Louis knew that. And so, by the way, did Brad – deep down."

"I've never understood how women can be shocked when they are cheated on by men who have proven themselves to be cheaters," Mom said. "If you marry a dog, you shouldn't be surprised when he lifts his leg on your rhododendron, sheds all over your black cashmere and buries an old smelly meat bone in your bed."

"Mom, please don't compare men who cheat to dogs," I said. "You know I happen to be very fond of dogs."

"And not so fond of men who cheat, I take it," Frannie said.

"Who is?" I said.

"The women who cheat with them, I guess," Frannie shrugged, taking a gulp of her beer.

"Life is still a big game to you, isn't it Frannie?" Mom said.

And with that comment, the levity left the evening and never returned. Frannie and Mom both got very quiet for quite a number of minutes, wondering, I'm sure, how best friends who had virtually always understood each other had grown to two such separate points. Frannie spent the rest of the evening directing her words to me.

"Speaking of men, Beth, you must have to fight them off."

"Not really, no," I said.

"Well, the right one will come along," she said. "I can remember when you were just a baby. You were such a pretty little thing. Hair like threads of gold. And you had a doll baby that looked just like you. You would never go anywhere without her. You called her Penny, do you remember that? I remember it like it was yesterday. And you would tell this big huge story about how Penny's Daddy is an airline pilot and was in Hawaii or Australia or Canada and would be coming home soon, bringing lots of toys. You took such good care of that baby doll, Beth. It was the cutest thing. I thought for sure you'd grow up to have a houseful of kids. I guess you just haven't found Mr. Right yet, huh? Or do you prefer the single life?"

"I prefer it," I said.

Frannie looked as if she didn't believe me. Can't blame her any. I didn't believe me either. I don't want to end up like Frannie. I want my mother's life. Exhausting and full. I felt a deep, piercing sadness that I would never have it.

"Wait, didn't your mother tell me you were seeing a special someone, Beth?"

I shrugged and looked at Mom.

"And where is he now?" Frannie asked.

"I don't know," I said. "Probably at home."

"Well, where ever he is, that's where you ought to be, Beth. I can see in your face that you love him madly."

Mom and Frannie left just after 10 o'clock. I shoved the wadded up sandwich papers into a plastic garbage bag, deposited our three half-full beer glasses in the sink and got in my car. I hadn't told Danny yet about John's dream. He would surely understand what it means. I had put off telling him because I didn't want him to use it against me. He would consider it proof that I should open my life to the possibility of children. I am not ready to do that. But I am ready to open my life to the possibility of him.

This is essentially what I had planned to tell him when he opened his door and found me on his porch step, holding a canvas wrapped in brown paper. He stared without speaking, as if trying to determine if I were an illusion. The warm light inside his house backlit his muscular body and tinged his white undershirt a creamy yellow. I wanted to press my face against that shirt every night and every morning for the rest of my life.

"What exactly are you trying to say, Beth?" he asked softly, brushing my hair from my face with his bent knuckle. My words had come out vague, just as I had intended them.

I grabbed his hand and pressed it against my face. "I'm not sure, exactly, " I said. "I am not sure about anything. Except this one thing. I don't want to go through life without you. So --" I looked down at the ground. He lifted my chin and peered into my eyes.

"If you still don't mind it being you and me, for the rest of our lives. I mean, if you still want to --" I took a long breath. "I will marry you, Danny. If the offer still stands."

He grabbed me and hugged me so hard, my feet left the ground. I don't think I've been hugged like that since Aunt Lily died. And then he took my hands and guided me to the porch

175

step, where we sat talking about the future, our shoulders wrapped in the golden light pouring out of his open door.

# Epilogue

# Chance of Icing

It has been a very long time since I wore make-up, panty-hose and high heels for an occasion other than a funeral. This day, for a change, presents a happy occasion, and I don't resent the discomfort. Actually, no. This is much more than a happy occasion. This is a sacred day, and all of nature seems to know it. This is not always the case in Seattle, but today the sun shone from the very moment it rose. I step out onto the porch to feel its graceful mingling with the gentle breeze. A dangling curl brushes against my freshly powdered cheek and I know I am beautiful, just as Danny told me on our first date. I wonder if he had a hand in calling down such clement weather. Had he prayed that this momentous day would be marked with the dream-like qualities of fairy-tale weather? It is, I think, a sign that God is pleased to bestow the sacrament.

At the threshold of St. James Cathedral, I am grateful to my mother. She made me learn Latin. That proved very helpful in my veterinary science studies, but also at this very moment, when I am able to decode the inscription over the door to St. James. "*Domus Dei, porta choeli.*" "House of God, Gate of Heaven."

A trumpet and drum announces the commencement of the procession at the enormous Cathedral, and the assembly sings with a bold voice:

*"Day of grace and day of favor, day of mercy from above, mystery of our redemption, gift of God's abundant love.*

*See, your children come before you; for a newer grace they pray. Consecrate them to your service, let them feel your love today."*

Danny's eye catches mine and he smiles. He proceeds down the aisle with four other men, hands clasped before them, marching reverently toward the holy moment. I keep my eye fixed on Danny as he takes his place near the altar. The liturgy unfurls like a magnificent tapestry, woven one thread after another by human hands, into a masterpiece with the unmistakable signature of God. You can almost see the soaring of souls, expanding and ascending toward the massive dome.

"Let Daniel Cicero DiCiccio, who is to be ordained Priest, come forward," the Bishop says.

A strange turn of events has transpired to get Danny to this very unusual place before the Bishop.

At some point in the course of helping me leave my past behind, it dawned on Danny that he had carried his with him, creating a vague feeling of unworthiness that covertly altered the options he had placed before himself.

There was a time, long ago, when Danny knew for certain that he had a vocation. He had heard the call. He had answered it. Nothing before or since had made him happier than that moment when he knew he heard it. Not even finding the person he considered the world's most beautiful woman, healing her 20-year-old nearly-incurable wound and getting her to agree to spend the rest of her life with him in the bonds of holy matrimony. Danny was meant for the priesthood, a fact he had forgotten until a certain day not long before I finally discovered I wanted to marry him.

It was the day Danny went to Confession with our long-time family friend, Father Fitz. Mom had asked Father Fitz to say a Mass for the repose of Lily's soul on the one-year anniversary of her death. After Mass, we all went to witness Father Fitz bless the new shelter I opened with Pablo's money in Rainier Valley. We named it Lily of the Valley Animal Shelter.

We all went to my parents' house for lunch after and somehow (I never learned the details) Danny ended up going to Confession in the back yard as I washed dishes, glancing out occasionally through the kitchen window. They must have been out there for a good 45 minutes or more, as I had time to wash, dry and put away plates and silverware used by thirty-two people and go back and scrub two large pots and a roasting pan that had needed to soak. Dad went to confession after that. I wondered if he was telling Father what he had told me on the day of Lily's funeral.

Upon his return indoors, Father Fitz asked me if I wanted to confess also, but there was no way I could tell another living soul, besides Danny, what I had done. So I told Father I needed to hurry and get to my animals because I had no volunteers scheduled for the afternoon.

The next day, I awoke with a picture in my mind of Danny bowing his head in the broad daylight of a suburban backyard, making the sign of the cross in the shadow of Father Fitz's hand, raised in absolution over Danny's head. In my sleepy state, somehow, in my interior, I saw the beauty of Danny's soul, like I had never seen beauty before. I felt such an overwhelming affection for Danny, that I was certain I could not live my life without him. I beat down my desire, knowing I could not give him children and not wanting to see a soul as beautiful as his wasted on a life with me. I decided never to see him again.

It wasn't until a month later, the day I learned of John's dream, that I began to understand that my soul could be beautiful again as well. Mercy could restore it to its original luster. And so, emboldened by my brush with Heaven, and repulsed by the utter desolation that Gregory Hill had to offer, I sought out the one who had done the most to help make me whole and endeavored to embark on a plan to keep him with me always.

There, on his porch step, I told Danny I didn't want to live without him. That's when he told me that he had spoken to Father Fitz during confession about the calling of his youth, and, after his absolution, he felt like his old self for the first time in twenty years. He then went home and fell asleep on the couch and had a dream about Lily. She told him all of Heaven was waiting for him to feed the hungry the Bread of Angels.

"I can't describe the elation I felt as I awoke from that dream, Beth. I will never be able to describe it as long as I live."

Although I didn't like the idea of Danny becoming a priest the first time I heard it, I have come to embrace it. Instead of feeling the loss of Danny, I feel a gain of joy, like a kingdom's citizen, watching a coronation and finding cause to rejoice in the installation of new royalty. Even though I myself will never see the inside of the palace, I know full well I will benefit, nonetheless, from the benevolence of the king.

"In the early part of this century," the Bishop begins his homily, "a former pastor of this magnificent church once wrote that the embrace of any cathedral should be wide. Sooner or later, people of all faiths and no faith at all find their way to it. A priest must also have a wide embrace. And I know that's what these five men, standing before you, bring to the priesthood. They come to this vocation from a wide range of backgrounds, with an impressive variety of life experience. Among them are a plumber, an engineer, a psychiatrist, a computer programmer and a widower with five grown children and a dozen grandchildren."

I look behind me into the massive sea of souls gathered in the pews to see if I can determine who his children and grandchildren might be. I think about how delighted they will be to receive Communion from the hands of their grandfather. I think about Pablo's hands – boney and veiny, but steady even until the day he died.

"My dear people," the bishop continues, "let us pray that the all-powerful Father will pour out the gifts of Heaven on these servants of his, whom he has chosen to be priests."

A lump forms in my throat as Danny and the other four candidates lay prostrate on the marble floor.

*Lord be merciful.*
*Lord save your people from our sin.*
*Lord save your people from everlasting death.*
*Lord save your people.*
*Be merciful to us sinners.*
*Lord, hear our prayer.*
*Jesus, son of the living God.*
*Lord, hear our prayer.*

In complete silence, at least 150 priests in white chasubles file past the five men, laying their hands on them, praying for the gift of the Holy Spirit in their service as priests.

The bishop presents each new priest with a paten and chalice, and a commandment: "Model your life on the mystery of the Lord's cross."

Danny will be receiving my gift in the mail. It is the second painting I had done since Lily's death – a lamb being pulled from thickets by a shepherd's staff, emblazoned near the hook with IC XC, the Greek initials for Jesus Christ. I titled the painting, *Mercy has a Name.* It is a companion piece to the one I gave Danny on his front porch that night I came to tell him I would marry him. That one depicts a lamb in dusky darkness outside a sheepfold, looking in at a brightly illuminated scene of a flock of sheep encircling the Good Shepherd, gazing up at him adoringly. I titled it *Seeking Mercy* and signed it, *From the woman who loves you.*

ೞೢೱೞೢೱೞೢೱೞೢೱೞೢ

I am one of this novice priest's first penitents and he is my first confessor – to my memory anyway. It takes thirty minutes in the confessional to outline the large and small regrets that have formed the unconscious basis for every decision I have made in my gristly life. Danny has heard all my sins already, but this time, he is able to offer me even more than understanding and advice. By virtue of his ordination and the purple stole draped around his neck, he is able to grant me freedom.

"God, the Father of mercies, through the death and resurrection of His Son, has reconciled the world to Himself and sent the Holy Spirit among us for the forgiveness of sins." Danny's hand rests gently on my head. "Through the ministry of the Church, may God give you pardon and peace. I absolve you from your sins in the name of the Father and the Son and the Holy Spirit. Amen."

"Amen," I say, making the sign of the cross. "Thank you, Father."

He smiles at me and takes my hand. "See you Saturday."

"Two-thirty," I say. "Or two."

"I'll be there at 2:15," he winks. "Sharp."

I smile at his recognition of my tribute to Aunt Lily. Years after her death, he still remembers. It is that kind of thing that preserves the bond between us -- the places and spaces within our common memories, some of which only he and I know.

When Danny went away to seminary, I felt abandoned and defeated. Was this really the way this was supposed to end? All that labor, all that moving forward was for him, because of him. He was the one who forced me through it. It had been so much work. Painful and grueling. Danny was the only one who knew me, through and through. And he still accepted me. I was finally to the point where I could consider marrying him. And what was it all for?

Of course, there had remained open the chance we would eventually end up together. Plenty of men who go to seminary never end up becoming priests. So I began to attend Mass regularly, so I might be at least somewhat suitable to be the wife of a former Seminarian, if that's the way it was going to turn out. I did so to share in the interests of my beloved -- to make the thing most important to him important to me. But, I have to say, I found great comfort in the Mass, far beyond the knowledge that it might one day be something I would share with Danny. There was a depth within its confines that I had found no place else in life.

I continued to write to Danny, determined to keep contact with him, to keep current the prescription for my woundedness. Danny's compassion was like a salve, which I still needed from time to time. I needed it so badly one time, that I made a trip out to see him at St. John Vianney Seminary in Denver during visitors' week. There was another visitor there that week to see his little brother. We enjoyed chatting over a cup of coffee after Mass one morning. We exchanged contact information and I returned home. Now I had e-mails and letters going out to Danny in Denver and Michael in Phoenix.

I might have been picturing Michael writing his e-mails to me from a hogan surrounded by tumble weeds and Saguaros, except I happened to already know a bit about Phoenix. Laura had won an all-expense-paid trip to the dry and sunny city when we were teenagers. She garnered first place in a nationwide essay contest on water conservation. We laughed at the irony of it all when we pulled up to our five-star resort and saw a mister system going full blast outside the lobby doors. That mister proved a week of trouble for us. Three-year-old John was the first to realize that it was just as much fun to dance in the Phoenix misters as it was in the Seattle rain. Actually, even more fun since it did not involve the chattering of teeth. The biggest problem with John's discovery was that he introduced the practice of mister dancing to Lily. And while it is easy enough to pick up and whisk away a 3-year-old when it's time to move on to another activity, it is impossible to do so to a heavy-set woman in her early 40s. And that particular woman would never have gotten enough of mister dancing, even had we let her go on until the leopard and the lamb lie down together. So, there they were, a very small boy and a rather chubby woman, giggling hysterically, alternately leaping in random patterns and then spinning in frenzied circles, faces pointed up into the fog. And this is what had to happen every time we came and went from our hotel.

Toward the end of our week there, we grew in wisdom and made like the locals, who never go anywhere in the summer. We opted to spend our time poolside, getting brain freeze from frozen drinks served in wide-mouthed glasses with tiny paper umbrellas. Anyway, it was much better than getting into our 150-degree rental car.

After having experienced Phoenix in August, I was relieved when Michael asked to come visit me instead of inviting me out his way. We sat out on my back porch, drinking sugar-laced espresso from Chinese tea cups – the kind with no handles – and talking about the smartest dog breeds and debating the superiority of the scorching, dry heat of the Arizona desert to the soppy Seattle heat wave. All the while, Bruce laid his head in Michael's lap to get his ears scratched. Not since Lily had that dog let anyone touch his ears.

It was well past midnight when Michael said goodnight and headed to his hotel. The next morning, I awoke late to find him out in the yard, laying bricks and digging holes. He said he knew I wouldn't mind if he employed his talents as a landscape architect to woo me with a barbeque grill and butterfly garden. He wanted me to think of him whenever I ate a hamburger or spotted a swallowtail. It worked, but it was unnecessary. I thought of him all the time – even when I ate things that could not be grilled, like oatmeal and banana cream pie, and even when I saw things that could not fly, like paint-chipped porch chairs and espresso machines.

When I said yes to his proposal, I thought his feet might never touch the ground again, even though I made it clear that, to my nearly unvacillating relief, my fertility has shown signs of winding down and there may be no children in our future.

When a person reaches a certain age, he comes to accept the very real possibility that he may never find true love. Children would have been icing on the cake for Michael, but he is happy enough just to have cake. With the remote chance of icing. He just kept saying that, if the Lord means for us to have children, we will, regardless of what we have to say about it. There've been more than a few women who have gotten pregnant unexpectedly, he reminded me, or who one day find themselves sitting in a court of law, waiting for a judge to ratify an adoption.

Who am I to argue that God's ways are ever predictable? I still remember what Danny said to me after his ordination, standing on the steps outside St. James. We were two matchbox-sized souls in the shadow of the Cathedral's twin bell towers, set a good fifteen stories up into the blue sky.

"See how mysterious our lives are, Beth. Had I not fallen in love with you, I may never have been a priest."

That was the first time I'd ever heard him say he had fallen in love with me. The words tugged at something deep within me. I had come to assume I was a project or a distraction for a man suffering from a phobia of commitment owing to a well-earned distrust of women. But now I believe Danny really did love me. He wasn't running away from something when he ran to the priesthood. He was running to something. He gave up something beautiful for something splendid. No one can blame him for that.

So, here I stand with my hand on the confessional door knob, thinking about the best way to tell Danny how much I'll miss him. He is leaving after he officiates his first wedding Mass on Saturday afternoon. He is bound for Haiti, having received permission to take a missionary assignment in an orphanage there.

"You are going to make a beautiful bride, Miss Lovely," he says. "Lovely, Lovely lady."

"Not Miss Lovely for much longer," I say, raising an eyebrow.

"But always, *always* lovely," he smiles. "See you Saturday."

As I leave the confessional, I have the profound realization I am not stepping out, but stepping in. I am entering a new world. Different, not because it has changed, but because I have. I choose a pew in the back of the church and kneel to pray a Rosary, which has been assigned me for my penance. I pull my grandmother's red rosary beads from the zipper compartment of my purse. Mom lent them to me for my "something borrowed." I pray the Apostle's Creed and an Our Father. After the first Hail Mary, I stop.

"Come closer."

Those are the words I hear, somewhere inside my head. I stand up and start down the center aisle, my eyes fixed on the wooden crucifix next to the altar. I am pulled past pew after pew, until I reach the steps of the sanctuary. I fall on my knees before the tabernacle and stretch out my hands, bathing in the light pouring in from the sky through the *oculus dei*, "the eye of God." There I am, very small, like a child, in the sight of the boundless, living God. And for the first time in my adult life, I have no shame. I stay there for some time, finishing my Rosary, basking.

Then, as I make my way past the enormous marble columns, back to the entrance of the church, I stop to dip my fingers in holy water, reading the inscription surrounding the baptismal font.

"*…that you may declare the wonderful deeds of God who called you out of darkness into marvelous light.*"

I bless myself and turn to look one more time at the Cathedral, hoping to commit to memory, not so much its stunning architecture, but its wide embrace.

"This is where I will raise my children," I hear myself whisper, without having planned to say it.

Like I said before, there were a number of unforeseen benefits to a life entwined with Aunt Lily's. Perhaps the greatest of these -- my friend and confessor, Father Daniel DiCiccio.

**About the Author**

Sherry Boas began her writing career in a hammock in a backyard woods in rural Massachusetts when she was eight years old, writing a "novel" about the crime-fighting abilities of her Cocker Spaniel. Fourteen years later, she would draw her first writer's paycheck for a very different kind of story when she landed a job at a newspaper in Arizona. She spent the next decade as a journalist, winning news awards, but her heart still belonged to fiction. So, after twelve years at home with her four adopted and highly inspiring children, the words to the Lily trilogy found themselves onto these pages. *Life Entwined with Lily's* is the final in the trilogy, following *Until Lily* and *Wherever Lily Goes*, also available from Caritas Press. Visit www.LilyTrilogy.com.